The Soft Detective

The
Soft Detective

H. R. F. Keating

Thorndike Press • Chivers Press
Thorndike, Maine USA   Bath, England

This Large Print edition is published by Thorndike Press, USA and by Chivers Press, England.

Published in 1998 in the U.S. by arrangement with St. Martin's Press, Inc.

Published in 1998 in the U.K. by arrangement with Macmillan Publishers Ltd.

U.S. Hardcover 0-7862-1565-8 (Thorndike Mystery Series Edition)
U.K. Hardcover 0-7540-3523-9 (Chivers Large Print)
U.K. Softcover   0-7540-3524-7 (Camden Large Print)

The text of this Large Print edition is unabridged.
Other aspects of the book may vary from the original edition.

Set in 16 pt. Plantin by Rick Gundberg.

Printed in the United States on permanent paper.

British Library Cataloguing in Publication Data available

Library of Congress Cataloging in Publication Data

Keating, H. R. F. (Henry Reymond Fitzwalter), 1926–
    The soft detective / H.R.F. Keating.
        p. cm.
    ISBN 0-7862-1565-8 (lg. print : hc : alk. paper)
    1. Large type books. I. Title.
    [PR6061.E26S65   1998]
    823'.914—dc21

98-28344

The Soft Detective

Chapter One

With the personal radio message headed *Fatal* in his hand, Detective Chief Inspector Benholme heard Sergeant March's voice through the open door of the CID Room. She sounded, as always, as if she was shouting down a stroppy bunch of yobbos.

'What's he like, the DCI? I'll tell you: soft as a duck's arse.'

He checked himself.

Best not to go in right on top of that. Not that it's going to embarrass March, me overhearing. Embarrassment and Di March poles apart. But one of the aides, newly arrived today, must have been asking about me and for them it would be awkward enough.

And is it true? Me, soft?

No, it's not. I suppose she has got a bit of a point. I've never gone in for Phil Benholme right or wrong. Can always see the other point of view. Which, damn it, makes me a good detective, gets me into witnesses' minds, criminals'. But . . . Well, there's a flip side to it. Vicky, would she and I still be together if I'd stopped myself always seeing her side? If I'd said bluntly *You married a copper, you've got to put up with what goes with that, long hours on duty, sudden call-outs?* Instead, when she went waltzing off, she must have thought ever-understanding Phil's going to understand this.

And she did have a lot to put up with, after all. Not only the lonely evenings, just her and young Conor, with him often tucked up in bed. Not just the unexpected extra hours, the outings cancelled at short notice. But times like, back when I was a DC and attended the corpse of that woman her husband had mutilated, and wasn't able to make love for two whole months afterwards.

Yet if when she went on at me I'd shot back in the same way, given her the no-question-I-am-right response, would that really have kept the marriage going? God knows.

And should I be equally tough in the job? Hard-arsed? Slam out orders, hell with reasons. There's plenty of senior officers do. But, no. No, damn it. No, I run a good ship, way I am. I do think of others, their reactions, what they must be feeling. And it makes the CID all the better. More bloody efficient.

So, you're wrong, Detective Sergeant March. My way something you should think about, if you ever think about anyone but yourself. And perhaps you do. Occasionally.

He went forward.

And, almost inside the door, realized that, if no one else in the room had seen him standing there, DI Carter at his desk at the top certainly had. And was enjoying the situation. Remnants of a smile on his face. And he'll be watching to see how I react. See if, say, I send March down to this fatal he's got his copy of. By the look of it just some poor old geezer conking out. See if I use it to get back at March? Do the put-'em-in-their-place senior-officer act? Give her this tuppenny-ha'penny task so she'll learn some respect.

But, no, damn it, I won't. No. I'd thought this barely worth sending a DC to. And I'll stick by that. Bob Carter or no Bob Carter. Discipline fanatic, see no further than his nose.

In the room he went straight over.

'Bob, this fatal down in Sandymount, I think we'd better just have a look-see. Bad area, after all.'

'Yeah. Was going to suggest it. Got plenty

of bods with nothing better to do this happy morning.'

Outside, fog swirling densely up from the river mouth as so often in King's Hampton had reduced everything to blotchy grayness.

'Well, Phil, who d'you want sending?'

Hint of malice in that too-innocent look.

'Oh, just any DC. Or, wait, no. No, might be something for one of the new aides to cut their teeth on.'

He paused.

'And in that case you'd better give it to March if she's not tied up. Needs someone who knows their way about, show them how the job should be done.'

'Oh, March is free all right. I'd sent her along to that big rally in the Town Hall last night, neo-Nazis, neo-Fascists, whatever those black-mac stirrers call themselves. Thought she might be able to pick out some of the thugs been causing trouble in the town. No go, of course. But her report, all neatly typed up, on my desk first thing. You know Miss Efficiency.'

Carter sent a swift glance down to the other end of the room where Di March, tall, well built (as they say), mass of auburn curls cascading down to her shoulders, dressed a bit butch in jeans and leather jacket, sat talking in low tones to the new female aide.

Now there was more than the hint of a smile on his heavy-jowled face.

Hell with him. Sending an aide to this little task under the eye of the only DS available the sensible thing to do. So do it. And never mind steamroller Bob Carter. I'm not, as a matter of strict fact, getting at Di March, whatever Bob's smirking about.

An hour later, reading the minimally bare report radioed in by March, he began to think he should have a go at her after all. With good reason now. She had left looking sullen enough to have guessed her *duck's arse* remark might have come to his ears, and in consequence her message was almost a direct duplicate of the beat officer's, not one single new circumstance in it. A deliberate piece of insolence. Cocking a snook.

Right then.

He sent a brief reply telling March to stay where she was till he came, and went down for his car.

Go to the scene. First of all, get rid of whichever aide had attended. Don't want to give March a bollocking in front of a junior. Next, take a quick look round, note anything March should have reported, and point out to her just where she's gone wrong. All right, perhaps understandable she felt aggrieved at what she thought was a petty punishment. But no excuse for deliberately slipshod work. She's a good detective all right, stands no nonsense, gets to the heart of things. And I don't care a bugger if her comments at a briefing sometimes verge on lack of respect. But now she's gone too far. Not doing her job. All right, like as not there's no more to the business than that first report indicated. But she should have told me just why.

In the fog the trip took him almost twice as long as it should have done. But at last he neared the estuary and the sea beyond and heard the mournful foghorns of the ships waiting there. Into his mind there came vague pictures of huge prehistoric beasts calling to each other across wide steamy swamps.

So it was much later than he had expected when he pulled up outside number twelve Percival Road, a house, as far as he could make out in the murk, though badly in need of repainting something of an exception to the generally run-down appearance of the whole of the area. Once one of King's Hampton's pleasanter parts, since a traffic-thundering six-lane road was bulldozed along the banks of the estuary Sandymount had become almost derelict. Its big old houses had been sold, split up into flats, left neglected. Many were occupied by squatters. Others had been taken over by West Indians and a small crowded community of Pakistani families. In consequence the entire place was now a policing headache. Saturday-night violence, drunkenness and not a little drug dealing, all the way from selling teenagers a few Ecstasy tablets to crack cocaine.

But number twelve had no crazy array of bell pushes beside its door. No faces were peering from behind tattered curtains. No broken pushchairs, stolen supermarket trolleys or remains of bicycles littered the front garden. Even most of the path's pattern of black and red tiles was more or less intact.

He wondered why the place had survived so comparatively well.

With a nod to the constable who had originally reported the death, standing muffled up in his greatcoat just inside the old cast-iron gate, he made his way up to the front door. Finding it just ajar, with ears cocked for Di March's loudspeaker tones he entered a long, darkened entrance hall, furnished only by a display cabinet, a few tarnished museum-like objects dimly visible behind its dusty panes.

Then he heard that loud voice from somewhere in the gloom ahead.

'Look, we've given him long enough. I'm off. There's real crime to be detected out there, if anyone's got the guts to go after it. You stay on, laddie, and tell him whatever it is he's taken it into —'

But twice quite enough for overhearing things I shouldn't.

'Sergeant March, you there?'

As if I don't know. But keep up the fiction.

'Ah, here you are, sir.' A loudly muttered *at last*. 'It's the door at the end.'

It opened as he approached and one of the new aides poked his head out.

What's his name? Yes, Johns.

'So, beginning to learn the ropes, are you?'

'Yes, sir.'

'Right then. Just nip out to my car, and sit there in case I get any messages.'

Then into the room, to deal with sulky Sergeant March.

Yet it was not March who first claimed his notice. It was the dead man. Not that as a body his was in any way horrifying. It was, in fact, the very lack of signs of violence that held his attention. Although the big bookcase, which in falling had brought about the death, still lay on the head half

14

hiding a fringe of white hair, the whole body, tiny in size, looked perfectly tranquil. Curled up like a sleeping child's among the jumble of books spilt on the floor with light brown hands loosely clasped, it had the air of being a quiet little dressed-up monkey.

After a long moment he turned to March. 'Well, do we even know who he is?'

'Yes, sir, we do. Now. I got hold of a neighbour a few minutes ago. They're all our ethnic cousins round here and, as you can see, the old guy's some sort of Indian himself. But, from what I was able to make out, his name's Unwala. Unwala, would you believe?'

'I see,' he said, deciding not to rebuke March for *our ethnic cousins*. 'And do I gather Mr Unwala lived alone? You having to ask a neighbour.'

'Yes, sir. I reckon he was going to that bookcase to take something out, and brought the whole thing down on himself, tugging at it. You can see the shelves all round the room are jammed tight.'

True, long, waist-high bookshelves on either side of the fog-smeared french windows — cages of some sort on top of them — were packed tight with dingy-spined volumes by the hundred varied by a sprinkling of bright modern jackets. He began to go

15

over to see if the titles would give him an idea what sort of a person the dead man was, a thin chill stream of fog-tinged air reaching him from two small top windows as he got nearer. But he stopped, struck by a thought.

'Sergeant,' he said, 'has it escaped your attention that there are books scattered over the floor all round the body?'

'No, sir. I have got eyes in — No, sir, I did notice that.'

'And what inference did you draw?'

'Infer — Oh, God. God, yes. The bookcase on the floor can't have been as jammed up as the others or the books would have stayed in it. So it wasn't trying to pull one out that . . . But — Well, it could have fallen on him for some other reason.'

But while she had been speaking he had knelt by the body and taken a more careful look. It had made him come to an unnerving conclusion.

'Yes,' he said, 'there could be any number of reasons why a heavy bookcase like this might fall over. But, however it happened, the dent in this poor old fellow's skull should have come where the top edge struck him, and the bookcase is quite the wrong height for that. Besides which, if you look closely at the carpet here, there's what looks like a faint scrape mark.'

He got to his feet.

'No, Sergeant, the bookcase has been moved. Moved so it would seem this poor devil was killed in a chance accident. What we've got here, almost certainly, is a murder.'

Through the open top windows there came a single long sad foghorn hoot from out in the estuary.

Chapter Two

March, her cascade of curls seeming distinctly subdued, sent off to radio for the Scene-of-Crime team, Benholme began to prowl and peer in the grey, fog-obscured light. Faint scratching sounds coming from the cages on the wall bookshelves drew him over. Peering forwards, hands in pockets to avoid any touching, he saw each cage was occupied by mice. White mice. Oblivious of his presence, and of that of the tiny corpse on the floor, they scuttered to and fro endlessly rapidly eating, though there seemed to be little enough left for them. The cages, he noticed, had numbers in the hundreds on them, written in neat script on yellowing labels.

So, Mr Unwala a bit of an eccentric? Keeping these pets? Observing their little scampering lives?

But that name *Unwala*, it seemed to ring a faint bell. For a moment or two he puzzled about it, but soon gave up. If it meant anything, sooner or later it would come back to him. In the meanwhile . . . Whoever had killed the old man might have gone into the other rooms in the big old house, have left there traces of himself.

He set off to explore. A dining room, of course, in a place like this. But it showed every sign of years of non-use. Its flowered wallpaper was dimmed almost to nothingness. The bare heavy table was dull with a deep layer of dust, as was the mahogany sideboard on which stood a brass flower vase sprouting a bundle of withered, time-dried stalks. The kitchen, when he moved into it, showed no signs of anything untoward, nothing an intruder had broken or displaced. A faint lingering odour of oriental spices gave some evidence of daily use. Then, what estate agents call 'the usual offices', the term seemed right for this now vacant house. Again there were signs of use, a fairly recent application of floor polish and the air tangy with squirt-on toilet cleaner.

Going up a floor, the first room he entered, expecting to find a bedroom, turned out instead to be equipped as a small laboratory, though what sort of work it was designed for was beyond him. But there was a chemicals-stained bench and on it some retorts, a rack of test tubes and a brass-fitted balance under a square glass cover. In a corner stood a piece of gray-painted equipment, the purpose of which, again, baffled him. And, once more, there seemed to be no trace of any intruder. The other bedroom on this floor was also a laboratory, though this showed even fewer signs of active use than the one next door. On its workbench he saw places where the mouse cages below might once have been ranged, rectangles less dusty than the area round them.

So what had this Mr Unwala been up to? He must be, or have been, pretty well off to have bought all this apparatus. But what had he used it for? What was he still using it for when he met his death? Some hobby? Turning base metal to gold? Well, no. Perhaps years ago he had been some sort of scientific consultant, though it was hard to guess what he might have been advising on.

But, if he was in fact well off, would rumours have got about, round here in now seedy Sandymount? Had someone broken in to look for some talked-about cache of money? And had little Mr Unwala disturbed him?

But there had been no sign of forced entry. Could someone then have wheedled their way in? Someone pretending to be an unemployed vendor of items of household equipment? But, again, Sandymount was hardly the place for that sort of enterprise.

A quick look into the bathroom. Empty. Forlorn. Out of use. A long rust stain running down from one of the heavy brass taps of the big, lion-footed tub.

Up to the top floor, still puzzling.

Another bathroom, not as large as the one below and with less elaborate fittings. But it looked as if it had, unlike the other, been in regular use. A tablet of soap on the basin still faintly sticky. A towel damp to the touch. Next door he found a smaller bedroom than those on the first floor, a room he guessed that in days gone by would have been occupied by a servant. But now it held just one rather small single bed. An effort had been made to pull up the bedclothes on it, not very successfully.

So this must be where the old man had slept. A well-worn pair of plaid slippers, small enough to be a boy's, were half-tucked under the bed.

But why did he sleep here when there must be a larger bedroom looking out over the estuary? Perhaps the noise of continuous traffic on the throughway had driven him out?

It was only when he crossed the landing

and opened the door opposite that he understood the real reason. The room was almost pitch-dark, heavy curtains across its windows. But when, taking a ballpoint from his pocket he carefully clicked down the old-fashioned brass switch, the light from a single dim bulb in a parchment shade — could it be only forty-watt? — showed him a big brass-ended double bed, fully made up but plainly left long unused. Its faded puffy silk eiderdown was carefully in place, its pillows were marble-smooth but no longer white as they must once have been. Instead they were the yellow of long-unbrushed teeth.

So old Mr Unwala must once have been married, have slept beside his wife here. Then she must have died. And he, unable any longer to bear the sight of their shared bed, had set himself up in the little room over the way. Leaving untouched, unseen, this bed that looked even more deserted than his own one at home, duvet so decisively flung off just three months ago by his Vicky. Now no longer his Vicky.

And there were certainly no signs of anyone having entered this room before him. On the ornate rosewood dressing table, its mirror a mass of fuzzy starring, silver-backed items of a woman's toilet set lay, dust-obscured. And untouched.

When he got downstairs again he found the Scene-of-Crime team had arrived and most of its members were already at work. The photographer's flashbulbs were intermittently flooding the whole scene with sudden dazzles of cruel revealing light: worn carpet, old-fashioned roll-top desk, volume-crammed bookshelves, the mouse cages above them. The video operator's camera was already whirring, capturing the wretched scene with equal blank disinterest. Beside the body the Scene-of-Crime officers, in their pristine white bulging paper coveralls, putting plastic bags over the deep-dented head and tiny pale brown hands, seemed to transform the shabby room into some hallucinatory science-fiction illustration.

Just outside the doorway the police surgeon hovered, waiting for enough clothing to be removed from the corpse to be able to carry out his necessary, yet rape-like, rectal temperature-taking. Behind him the coroner's officer waited his turn, on the floor beside him the long body bag on its stretcher, looking absurdly too big for the little, battered to death monkey-form it was to contain.

'Boss,' one of the DCs called from beside

the french windows.

He went over.

'Boss, these doors are only just pulled to. Looks like whoever did it could have gone out this way. Don't suppose that poor little bugger there took a morning stroll in the garden, day like this.'

'I doubt if he did.'

He went over to the fingerprint officer, busy puffing his clouds of grey aluminium powder on every available surface, occasionally lifting a print on to sticky tape with a little rasping sound.

'Looks as if chummy went out by the french windows,' he said to him. 'Might get something from the latch. Or the bolts top and bottom.'

He turned and peered out through the windows at the fog-wreathed patch of garden. It was miserably desolate. What must once have been a long stretch of lawn, big enough in times long gone for croquet, was now a short ugly area of uncut tussocky grass. It was cut off a dozen yards from the house by a tall concrete-slab fence, no doubt erected when the throughway was built. Borders to either side still supported a few of the shrubs careful owners must have planted long ago. At the far end two clumps of sodden Michaelmas daisies made patches of pallid colour. Once, he thought, the people in this and the similar houses to either side must often on summer days, have gone out through gates at the foot of their gardens to picnic or paddle by the shore twenty or thirty yards away across a sandy track. Now from beyond the tall slabby fence there could be heard only the rumble of heavy-goods vehicles ploughing implacably along.

Turning away, he saw Detective Sergeant Hastings, solid, fattish, pink-faced, bald head fringed with fair hair, had arrived to organize door-to-door inquiries.

'Jumbo,' he called out to him. 'It looks now as if our man may have got away through the garden. Will you supervise a fingertip search first of all? You won't need more than a couple of sensible chaps, and some aides. It's a small enough area. With any luck we might turn up something. We've precious little to go on so far.'

Reminded by that, he asked the fingerprint officer if there had been any likely-looking prints on the heavy bookcase where it had been manoeuvred to rest improbably on the edge of the victim's head.

'You want to be so lucky. Anywhere chummy might have touched has been given a good wipe-over.'

'Telly got a lot to be blamed for,' he

answered wryly. 'If you had found a print, we could safely arrest the only man in the British Isles who doesn't know about dabs.'

The surgeon, he saw, had now finished and the coroner's officer was supervising putting the tiny, frail corpse into his anonymous body bag, the sound of its metal zip screechingly loud in the subdued atmosphere. He hurried out of the way before the stretcher had to be carried through the dreary hallway and stood on the front step, sucking in breaths of clammy fog.

'Who was it,' he asked the constable stamping his booted feet by the gate, 'you said in your message told you about this?'

'West Indian lady who drops in time to time to clean for the old man, sir. Name of Damberry, Mrs Damberry. Works in the corner shop at the end of the road.'

'Right. Yes, good man. If I'm wanted, that's where I'll be.'

Then he halted.

Should I take March with me? Been looking glum as a wet drum since she came back from calling in the SOCO team. Might make her feel she hasn't blotted her record for ever and ever.

He stepped inside again and called her. But as they made their way to the shop, the pavement under their feet chill and slippery, trees in the gardens sullenly dripping, she trudged along in unvarying silence. Gone all the belligerent glances she normally darted to left and right wherever she walked.

He racked his brains for something to say that might lift her ill humour. Found nothing.

Not, he thought, what they call a companionable silence.

From the river mouth came another long, sad foghorn hoot.

As they negotiated the flapping metal National Lottery sign standing outside the goods-crammed window of the corner shop, bright ads for cut-price offers pasted all over it, he did at last find something to say.

'Take care, when we see this lady, not to let her know we think it's murder.'

In acknowledgement March produced a single sharp sigh. Plainly saying *I am a detective, you know . . . sir.*

He cursed himself.

'Oh, poor, poor Mr Un,' Mrs Damberry, broad-beamed, mighty-bosomed, round-faced, said immediately he had introduced himself. 'You know, so soon as I saw that light on over his door on my way to work first thing this morning I knew something very wrong. Mr Un, he was always too, too careful of the electric. Just like poor Mrs Un before him.'

Mr Un, he thought. Mr Unwala. Where the devil have I heard that name before?

But Mrs Damberry, in generous flood, was going on. ' "Look after him, my dear". That what Mrs Un say when she went into the hospital. She knew she weren't never going to come out of there, and she worried sick the poor old man don't know how to take care of he self no more than a little child.'

'So when was that? Has Mrs Unwala been dead for long?'

'Oh, three year, come Christmas. Three year ago she went. So I said to myself there and then: every blessed Sunday when the shop ain't open in I'll go, give the place a turnout, see he got enough to eat in that kitchen, got clean clothes to put on.'

'Last Sunday? You were there last Sunday?'

'Every blessed Sunday I there. And right as rain little Mr Un was then. Right as blessed rain. And now . . . Now he dead, dead jus' like what I found him. Under that big, big bookcase. Always reading and reading in those big books of he, Mr Un. But each time I come in, up he look, smile on he little face. "Good day, Mrs Damberry, I trust you're quite well", he say. Funny old way he had to talk. Always the same.'

'So then, when you saw that light in the transom, you went in. You've got a key, I suppose?'

'Oh, yes. Mrs Un, she give me that. Mighty fuss that sister of her made when she hear I had it. But then she never set foot in that house, not more than once in a six-month, when Mrs Un was there. So she weren't never going to go there after she gone. I tell you that.'

'Ah, now, this lady, Mr Unwala's sister-in-law, is she the only relative he had? Or do you know of any others?'

Mrs Damberry decisively shook her head.

'Not one single blessed one, 'less he had some back in India where he ain't ever been in all the time I knowing Mrs Un, and that be plenty years I telling you.'

'And do you happen to know this sister, sister-in-law's name and address? We'll have to inform her, you know.'

'Don't know no address. But she call Polworthy. Mrs Polworthy. That I do know.'

He turned to March, stubbornly indifferent beside him.

'Make a note, will you, Sergeant. There shouldn't be too many Polworthys in the town. You could winkle her out in half an hour.'

Enough encouragement, give her back some self-esteem? Well, has to be. Can't spare more time than that.

And just one more question for Mrs Damberry.

'Tell me, did anybody else go to visit Mr Unwala? Anyone else that you know of?'

'No. Not one soul did he know, poor old man. Kept himself to he self. Well, he being different from most folks round here. But she weren't, Mrs Un. She a white lady liked to talk. How I got to know her, coming into the shop. And him. Sometimes she ask him to go for her.'

'But you can't think of anyone, anyone at all, who was in the habit of calling at the house? The vicar? Well, no, not round here, I suppose.'

'No, sir, no one calling, not to go inside, 'cept maybe what he telling me Sunday, some little boy help him catch one of they mice of he when it get out of its cage. But that front door stay shut nowadays all day long and all night too. Only —'

She stopped abruptly, as if she felt she should check at least for a moment the rush of her spoken thoughts. A moment to ask herself if she should say what she had been on the point of letting pour out.

'Yes?' he prompted. 'Only when?'

'Oh, well. Was jus' the one time. Funny thing, 'bout four, five week past.'

Behind him, he realized that March had cast off her gloom, at least to the extent of giving out signs of fretting impatience.

'Four weeks ago?' he said to Mrs Damberry. 'Well, I wouldn't worry about that. I doubt if anything that happened that far off would help us.'

But he had reckoned without his determined gossip. And, in the face of her relentless ploughing on, he did not quite like to turn away leaving her talking.

'I saying to myself after that a strange, strange thing. Month go by after month an' no one going inside that house 'cept me on a Sunday, and then this happen. There some funny goings-on in this world an' no mistake.'

'Some funny goings-on?' he asked, conscious of March resolutely turned to the shop door.

But with Mrs Damberry exuding, never mind her hosepipe gossipiness, such spreading goodwill he had been unable to abandon his question.

'Yes, sir,' she took him up quickly. 'That Sunday when I come. Mr Un still sleeping, way he sometimes do if I is good an' early. But that room of he, you should of seen.

Papers all over the floor. An' — Well, this I don't like to say. But pee. I know what pee smell like, an' I know what it look like on the floor. An' there it was, all over them papers. An' he ain't doing that. Not my nice an' quiet little Mr Un.'

He was paying full attention now. As, he realized, was March behind him.

'But this was four weeks ago? Or five, did you say? Not more recently? You're sure?'

'Four, five week, I said. Four, five week it was.'

'And did Mr Unwala have any explanation?'

'Yes, sir. And no.'

'Yes and no?'

'He in bed when I found him, an' I ain't sure but I think he got one damn nasty black eye in that little face of he. But "Please don't ask me about it, Mrs Damberry", he say. An' when he ask in that way, so nice an' polite, then I jus' don't ask. An' I ain't never done.'

'But it looked as if somebody had been in the house? Perhaps attacked Mr Unwala? Flung papers of his on the floor and urinated on them, is that it? Somebody or several people?'

'U-rine-ated. That the very word.'

He turned to March.

'What d'you think, Sergeant?'

But Mrs Damberry had more to say.

'I telling you what I think. I think it were that Hampton Hoard.'

'That old story,' March muttered.

'The Hampton Hoard,' he said to Mrs Damberry, ignoring her. 'I've heard a bit about that. My young son is something of an archaeologist. Or anyway a treasure hunter. Expensive metal detector. His hobby. But the Hoard's meant to be Celtic coins, right? One or two get picked up on the dunes every once in a while, and it's meant to be a sign there's a big hoard of them buried somewhere near, just waiting to be found. Worth thousands.'

'That be worth one million pound, sir. One million. That what folks round here be saying.'

'Well, I'm no expert . . . But have you got some reason for thinking whatever happened in Mr Unwala's house that time is connected to this hoard?'

'I sure an' certain have. Poor Mrs Un. She was one of them like that son of you. Archae-what-they-call-them. She goin' out on they dunes, finding all sorts old coin an' badges an' things. She show me once a coin she found. Gold. Pure gold, that what it was. She study all that when she weren't no more than a girl, you know. Cambridge University. Cambridge University. That where she met little Mr Un. Told me many a time.'

He remembered the dusty-paned cabinet in the hallway of the house. There had been coins among the objects displayed in it. So to that extent what big, fat Mrs Damberry believed might be the truth. If it had got about that Mrs Unwala had been a trained archaeologist, then the rumour might have spread that she actually knew where the Hampton Hoard was buried, although for some reason — her poor health? — she hadn't been able to dig it up. And eventually some local criminals might have decided she would have written down the magic location before her death. Had they forced or tricked their way into little Mr Unwala's house four weeks ago, searched his papers, found nothing? Attacked him when he heard them? And then did they come back last night intending to make the old man tell them what he knew? And had something gone wrong?

Evidently the same thought had occurred to March.

'You want me to have a look through any papers there are there, sir?' she said, suddenly all bright-eyed. 'We just might be on to something.'

He almost agreed. But no. After all, the whole thing depended on an altogether unlikely rumour. However much it was beginning to excite March. No, those next of kin — if that's what they were — they had to be found as soon as possible and told about the death. People were owed something.

He sent her off to the station, and its directories and files.

Mass of auburn curls soon swallowed up in the still persisting fog.

Chapter Three

Benholme did not go back into the house after he had at last parted from Mrs Damberry. His task now, in full charge of the inquiry in the absence of Detective Superintendent Verney on a Bramshill College course, was first to see that everything needed for a Major Incident set-up was in place. Then he had to put the team on it fully in the picture. Do more, however, than just dole out information. He would have to set light to a powder train to lead from relative ignorance to full knowledge of who the murderer was. No doubt in the hours and days ahead that powder train would twist and turn, would jerk and sputter, might on occasion seem to be on the point of damp extinction. But, well lit, it must in the end blaze up its target.

All seemed to be in order when, the faint greasiness of an early lunch of canteen sausages and chips clinging to his palate, he arrived at the Muster Room. On its normally bare stone floor half a dozen tables had been pushed together to make one long one. Already piles of big Action sheets had been put there ready to be filled in as the inquiry generated more and more tasked actions. Scattered here and there, almost equally necessary, were ashtrays in painted tin, glass, chipped earthenware.

At the top of the room under the large blackboard, which at straightforward times served a variety of purposes ranging from lectures to cadets to carefully colour-chalked Christmas greetings, a trestle table had been put up for his own use. In-tray and out-tray, notepads, bundle of ballpoints, telephone. Along one of the walls an electrician was installing the last of a bank of other phones. The screens of a row of computers were already glowing.

Uniformed officers, just in from the house-to-house inquiries, were standing in one corner, faces still red and raw from the foggy chill, voices muttering complaints. In another corner detectives in their current trademark leather jackets chatted more loudly, the word *overtime* in markedly hopeful tones emerging.

At the head of the long makeshift table Jumbo Hastings's weighty buttocks were planted on a folding chair looking hardly substantial enough for them. Three or four clip-in files, empty now, eventually to be cramfull, lay in front of him.

'Jumbo,' Benholme said. 'Here already? Your fingertip searchers in the garden come up with anything?'

'Produced a nice little task for that new aide, the glamour-puss one.'

'Hart. Maureen Hart. Called Mo, if I'm right. Yes?'

'That's the one. "Sergeant, Sergeant," she came up to me saying. "Someone's vomited down by the fence there. What shall I do about it?" So I told her. Nice fresh puke? Then put it in an evidence bag, sweetheart, every last scrap. Use those spiky red nails of yours if you can't find anything else.'

'Somehow I think she managed without spoiling the claws, right?'

'Right.'

'And it's off to Forensic? If it's down to our fellow and not some wandering idiot poking his head over the fence, might tell us something.'

'It's on its way.'

'Good man. Anything else?'

'Early days yet, guy. Though I did manage to squeeze out of the doc an approximate time of death. Somewhere in the early evening of Monday. To be confirmed, of course. And there was something else. Something that just might turn up trumps.'

'What's that then?'

'Footmark. In the muddy earth at the bottom end. It's not too clear, but it does make it look as if our fellow may have left that way. Would have had to get himself over the fence and made the footprint pushing himself up. If it is him he was wearing trainers, size seven or thereabouts. Just one foot, the right. Whoever it was left no other traces worth a bugger. The grass on that so-called lawn too thick for SOCO to get anything at all.'

'The footmark, you got it lifted?'

'No trouble. Ground just right. Bagged and tagged and off to Forensic. To tell us it's one sold by the thousand in Woolworth's.'

'I dare say. But size seven? Gives us something. It'll be someone small. Could be a woman even. Attack like this not what's generally seen as a woman's crime, but . . .'

Jumbo grinned.

'Women's rights these days though. Got to be politically correct.'

'More to the point, what's in from the house-to-house?'

'Come on, guv. What d'you expect? Miracles?'

'Something like that,' he answered cheerfully.

'The impossible takes a little longer,' Jumbo said, ever one for a well-used phrase.

'But not too long, eh?'

He began to move off.

'Guv, one other thing.'

Jumbo beckoned him nearer.

'I'd think it'd be a fair bet we'll still be here Saturday,' he said.

'Almost a cert.'

'So have you forgotten the piss-up planned for Saturday night, Bob Carter's fortieth?'

'Oh, shit. Yes. Some Toffs and Tarts thing, wasn't it? It'll have to be postponed, that's for sure. I don't suppose the lads will be too pleased but there it is.'

'Well, are you going to make an announcement? Or shall I just pass the word around?'

'No, Jumbo. My decision, I'll announce it.'

But a Toffs and Tarts party, he thought as he went up to the platform for the briefing. What an appallingly crass idea. Why is it the grottiness of CID work seems to produce a cruder, coarser outlook than the same people, women as much as men, would have if they'd got jobs as — what?

40

Schoolteachers, managers, secretaries? Di March make a good top PA, bossy, bold, super-efficient. But they all — well, almost all — are less thoughtful than if they'd not been in the police. Still, a brute mentality goes with a dirty job. Or so it seems.

Announcing the postponement made a poor start to the briefing. A worse one than he had reckoned on, failing to take into account his own dislike of what Jumbo had cheerfully described as a piss-up. There had been an immediate murmur of resentment, a restive exchange of glances.

He realized he had muffed it. The truth was that, as he had stood calling for quiet, the contrast between a Toffs and Tarts party and the investigation he was launching into that sad, solitary death had abruptly struck him. Little Mr Unwala, that monkey-like quiet corpse, head half concealed by the heavy bookcase dragged on to it, the dusty old house he had lived in, that bed left for years untouched — all had for a long moment come alive in his brain.

But they had not filled him with the kind of determination he had seen in other officers leading a murder inquiry. An uncluttered ambition to succeed when the eyes of the world were on them. A response to a challenge. A simple, rousing animal response.

41

A murder case becoming purely a personal crusade, to be resolved more quickly than any case before.

So the mild jokes he hastily contrived — *DI Carter'll have to stay thirty-nine till we've sorted this* — simply failed to quash the antagonism he felt swirling up. The atmosphere did not grow more cheerful. But, more important, he knew, too, he had done nothing to infuse his team with the plain determination to right a wrong which he felt in himself.

Well, he found he was thinking as he stood ploughingly outlining the details, it's understandable in a way, the resentment. That party's been long planned, much talked about. But no time now for idle speculation. My besetting sin. Or is it?

Come on, concentrate. And force yourself.

'Right then. A nasty business. And what I want is: I want it detecting. I don't want a single one of you to leave out one single detail of any task you're actioned with. One slip, one piece of carelessness, and this whole inquiry could go tumbling into dust. Remember that. Remember it, and good luck to you all.'

But when he asked for questions there were only two or three indifferent ones, hardly requiring answers. He realized with an inward sinking that, for all his late attempt to impose his will, he had still messed it up.

I want it detecting. But was there, is there, some lack in me that makes that demand so many empty words? Or at best half-empty? Have I not got in me all the brute will needed to trample my way to a result?

Something there I can't ever quite shuck off?

He stood watching while the room began to become a machine at work. Phones picked up. Computer keyboards tapped at. Jumbo Hastings, up at the big blackboard now, chalk squeaking, starting to allocate tasks on the few actions generated by what they had learnt already. Cigarette smoke beginning to drift upwards. Occasional sharp curses punctuating the hum of business as mistakes were made, corrected.

But, as he listened to it all, he felt himself becoming more and more convinced that everything was not as it ought to be. Unmistakably there was something lacking. The feel of a whole team working to one end.

The weight of their task ought to be in the head of everyone in the room, even if they were hardly conscious of it. But plainly it was not. The thought should be lending to their every least word or movement an extra of urgency. Fuelling the will to find this man. The killer. The man who had swept down some heavy object — but what? Nothing found so far — on to the white-haired skull of poor, innocent Mr Unwala.

That name again. Unwala. He had heard it before. He had. Somewhere. Somehow.

But scratch at his memory as he might, nothing came to the surface.

He shrugged.

And where now was that feeling he could recall from every other murder inquiry he had been involved in right from his earliest days as a detective and even before? The challenge of murder, the ultimate crime. The ending of another's life. Your own life, in a way, at stake if killers weren't caught, if you didn't get a result. Even the lives of everyone you knew. Your loved ones.

With a sudden pang he thought of Conor. The boy's precarious situation. Father and mother abruptly — as he at least must have seen it and felt it — torn away one from the other. All right, the boy seemed to have weathered it. A good lad. Head on his shoulders. He ought to do all right in the end. But . . . But underneath was something going wrong? It could be. It could be. With a boy of that age, sixteen next birthday after all, you couldn't expect to hear of every thought that entered his head. That stayed in his head. Stayed too long? Rotted there.

And Vicky? All right, she'd chosen to take the path she had. Into the arms of Mike, sporting hero. Or small-time sporting hero. No, be fair, a decent enough bloke. But, see her side, though she hadn't been absolutely pushed into Mike's arms, she hadn't been cherished enough for the temptation not to be there. Of Mike's ready arms in particular, or of any others hovering.

He let it go. Things to do. He looked around, saw March and beckoned her over. The way she was, she at least ought to be fired with keenness. Even if — another misjudgment perhaps? — in the shop earlier he had tasked her not with pursuing that faint Hampton Hoard lead as she wanted to, but merely with locating Mr Unwala's next of kin.

'Any luck finding those relatives? What were they called? Polworthy?'

'The only Polworthys in town. Report's in your tray.'

Rebuked. But, all the same, does she never think somebody may be too busy with other things to have read the report she has chosen to make? For a moment he wanted to snap *Say sir when you speak to me.* But he held back. After all, when she had first gone to the house she had made a bad mistake, and someone like her took making mistakes harder than most. She deserved a little leeway.

Nevertheless he scrabbled in his rapidly filling intray, found the report, noted the address, Frogs Lane.

And suddenly, because of that, he remembered what he had had in the back of his mind since he had got out of bed in the morning: that this was Tuesday. Tuesday. His day for going to see Conor in Mike and Vicky's flat. In — coincidence, coincidence — Frogs Lane. His day for going to make sure that Conor, when he'd got back from school, had got his tea, was doing his homework. Not necessary. The boy was capable of heating up a can of beans, whatever. And could be relied on, in fact, to do the homework. But this was Vicky's demand. Her harridan voice, as he sometimes called it to himself. *Christ, Phil, you might at least show some interest in the boy just once a week. Mike and I are entitled to some time on our own.* For her to watch her Mike playing football, rugger, squash, whichever it was.

But can I go out there now? With a major inquiry just starting up.

46

He thought about it. Uneasily.

Well, I might be able to fudge it. I have got to visit the Polworthys, after all. They deserve to be told about the death by the officer in charge of the inquiry. My duty, as I see it. But am I really right to combine that with going to see Conor? Still, perhaps I could cut looking in on him to the minimum. Say hello, tell him quickly what's happening and buzz off to the Polworthys', further along the lane to judge by the house number. He'll understand. Even if his mother wouldn't. Or not every time. Be fair.

Then Jumbo came up.

'Something from the house-to-house. Just got to it. Bit iffy, but might be something.'

His hopes flickered up. Would this at last be what was needed to enthuse the inquiry?

'Right. Let's hear it.'

'From a Paki lodging house, fourteen Percival Road, just a couple of doors along from the scene. Apparently a lady on the top floor there says she heard a scream. Or a shout. She thought it was "You black bastard". She's a Mrs Ahmed, a Pakistani, and the report says she wasn't too clear in what she was saying. But seems she's at least sure of the time. Just on six o'clock. She'd heard the weather forecast on ITV. More fog.'

'Well, they got that right. But could she

really be certain the shout — or scream, did you say? — came from the house?'

'Apparently she says it did. Something about the place in between being occupied by squatters out at that time of the evening. So she says it couldn't have come from anywhere else.'

'Well, action it, will you? Send someone reliable to see how much more they can get out of this Mrs Ahmed. And Jumbo, use someone who gets on with Pakistanis, for God's sake. Or she'll clam up a hundred per cent, and we'll lose this. And I've a notion it could be the lead we need. No, wait. Damn it, I'll go myself. You can hold the fort here, can't you?'

'Oh, yes,' Jumbo said, solidly confident.

He reached for his coat.

Just the job for me, in fact. Ability to get into the mind of someone different needed. A Pakistani woman. Yes, I ought to be the one doing this.

And easy enough to go on from the house there to the cottage in Frogs Lane. Couple of miles at the most. Then quick word with Conor, check he's all right. And on to see the Polworthys, not much further.

You black bastard. If that's what Mrs Ahmed really did hear, it could well have been the murderer yelling. Usual thing from

48

the doc about not being able to tell the time of death until the PM, but he had said *some time probably last evening.* So it would fit. Not a lot to go on, though. What sort of a voice had it been, shouting? Or screaming? But treat this Mrs Ahmed properly, the way I can, and with any luck I'll learn something more.

Chapter Four

Churning his car once again through streets which the fog and now oncoming darkness made doubly difficult, disconnected thoughts about the case came and went in Benholme's head. Twinges of anger with himself, too, at the way he had failed to fire up his team.

Was he even because of that failure going off at this moment on a wild-goose chase? Had he allowed hope to mislead him? Could this Mrs Ahmed really have heard those precise words, *You black bastard?* Or had she, nursing fears of racial abuse like many Pakistani women, heard in some quite neutral shout words she feared? When you thought about it, the circumstances were pretty unlikely. To hear a shout amid the sort of noise you might expect in that part of the town at that time of day must itself be a matter of pure chance. And then to put actual words to it . . . And how had Mrs Ahmed been able to tell just where it

50

had come from? How, even, had she managed to hear it at all from right inside number twelve?

But if she had in fact heard the shout — the scream? the yell? — and had heard those words correctly, what was the implication? Surely that little Mr Unwala had been the victim of a casual attack?

For some reason or other — But what? — he might have opened his front door and some passing racist yobbo had then taken it into his head to pick on him. And in the end it had gone too far. That could be something that might happen. Hadn't Mrs Damberry mentioned a little boy once helping the old man catch one of his mice? So he did sometimes open his door.

And then there was that business of the scattered papers and Mrs Damberry's *u-rine-ated*. That could have been the same sort of incident. It could have had nothing to do with the absurd rumour of the million-pound Hampton Hoard. It could be a case of unthinking racist violence.

Which if we do eventually get a result, he thought, will bring problems of its own. We may not have the trouble big cities with black populations have, but we're not without our share of racial antagonism. Like those so-called Britforce people.

51

He nosed his way past Mr Unwala's house, looking, he thought, like some giant parcel with the coloured plastic *POLICE — CRIME SCENE — POLICE* ribbons strung across it. A PC on duty outside stood flapping his arms for warmth. At number fourteen, which in contrast to number twelve was a total mess, he pulled up. In the patch of beaten-down earth that once had been its front garden lay a battered old pram with a hole in its underside, two or three half-rotten wooden crates, half a dozen tramped-down cardboard cartons. And, as was to be expected, the door of the house stood wide open.

Making his way up the stairs, pungent with spicy cooking smells, he had to stop at each landing to explain and argue his way past lounging, loudly talking Pakistanis spilling out of the rooms. At last he reached Mrs Ahmed's attic.

Behind its flimsy door he could hear a thin stream of tinny TV cartoon music. He knocked. The door was opened just a few inches. Mrs Ahmed, he saw, was an intent-looking, nervy woman of perhaps fifty, sharp-nosed, wary-eyed, a worn-looking orange and green cotton sari wrapped tightly round her.

He introduced himself but had to show

her his warrant card — her English, once he was attuned to it, a good deal better than the PC's report had indicated — before she ceased to look ready to bang in his face the little door crammed under the roof. Patiently he told her as much as he thought he should about the circumstances of the murder. Then at last her suspiciousness melted enough to allow him in.

As he ducked inside he understood why her claim to have heard a shout from a house two doors along might after all not be impossible. The room's one tiny window was evidently too ancient to be opened. But in the sloping ceiling there was a skylight. And, despite the chill of the night, it appeared to be permanently propped up. So a shout from number twelve might well, through the open top windows above the mice cages there, have reached this attic. Sound carries.

'Tell me, if you would,' he said, as mercifully she turned down the volume on the little black and white TV perched on a flimsy table in one corner, 'about this shout, or scream, you told the constable you had heard. Were you in here at the time? Did it come through the skylight there?'

'Where else? Are you thinking I was making this-all up? Not at all. I was hearing that scream. Definitely. I am not hearing sounds from that house before, but I am knowing and knowing that is where that scream was coming from.'

'But — really I don't mean to doubt you — how is it you're sure it didn't come from the house next door, or even from the one further along?'

'No, no. I am very much right. Next door is squatters. I do not like, but . . . And also they are out always till late in evening. So, not those people. No. And from far along, not possible. If I could hear noises they are making there, I would have heard before. But, no, never.'

So not as unlikely as he had thought. Far from it.

'That seems very clear,' he said. 'You're being a great help. But tell me again, what did this person who shouted, or screamed, say? You could make it out fairly clearly?'

'Oh, yes. Just what I was telling the policeman who came. I am certain-certain. It was "You black bastard". Yes, those words, very loud, and no others. You know, I have not seen the gentleman who lived in that house many times — he is not often going out, I am thinking. But, yes, he is black, as they are calling it. I think he is Indian gentleman.'

'Yes, he is. So I understand. But you told the officer who saw you this afternoon that it was not a shout but a scream you heard. Is that right?'

She stood for a moment thinking, lips pursed.

'Yes,' she said eventually. 'Much more of scream than shout. Some boy very angry, frighten even.'

'Boy, you say? A boy's voice, but what age of boy? You're sure it was a boy?'

'Yes, yes. I am knowing what is sounding like a boy.'

'So what sort of age? When you say boy, it could be any young man, isn't that right? Isn't that how you describe young men where you come from?'

'Oh, yes, sir. A young man is a boy until he is married, we are saying.'

'So this was a young man?'

'No, no. This was a boy-boy. Definitely. Some young boy was killing that old man. Disgraceful.'

'But what sort of age? Take your time in answering. This may be very important.'

Could the killer really be what she had called a boy-boy? A teenager? Or even younger? Well, boys of that age had been known to commit murder in the course of breaking into a house where there was an old person. And Mr Unwala would hardly have been able to put up much of a fight.

'Yes,' Mrs Ahmed pronounced eventually.

'Well?'

'Fourteen, fifteen years. More if the voice very late broken. Some very very bad boy.'

'Thank you. You've been most helpful. Perhaps at some future date we may have to ask you to give evidence in court. Would you be happy about that?'

'Yes.'

Again a firm note of decision.

A few clearing-up questions more and he made his way down the broken-banister stairs and out into the now blackly dark evening.

Sitting in the car jotting down what he had learnt in his pocketbook, he decided it was almost certain the murder had come about in the way he had envisaged earlier. For some reason little Mr Unwala must have had his door open when, surely, some racist yobbos had gone past. And they had pushed him inside, begun some rough-house horse-play, and then something Mr Unwala had said, some protest he had made, had lit to fury one of the younger members of the gang. Who had shouted out *You black bastard.* At almost exactly six o'clock. Mrs

Ahmed had been as definite about the time as about anything else. Just after hearing the twenty-to-six news. Confirmation of the time of death still to come from the pathologist but, unless that flatly contradicted Mrs Ahmed, a 'boy' had been there in the house then and had yelled *You black bastard.* Presumably just before he, or one of the other yobbos with him, had lashed out.

With what? Nothing found at the scene.

So, one thing. As soon as it was daylight all the verge of traffic-thundering Seabray Way would have to be searched. If that size-seven footmark had been left as the lot of them were making their getaway, then they must have taken the murder weapon with them. Whatever it was.

Find that. Find fingerprints on it, and we'll be more than halfway there.

And, another thing, call up on the computer the names of every young tearaway on the files. Detectives out and about as soon as the names were known, round to every address. This evening if possible. Check each one's whereabouts on Monday evening, have a look at the youths themselves if they're not out in the town. There'll be signs of uneasiness there, almost for a cert. No one as young as that boy who shouted can have done that and still be totally unconcerned. Or only one in ten thousand.

And — *youths, boys, young Conor* — quickly drop in on him. No more than a couple of minutes there, then on to the Polworthys. Pity I've got to take time for them. But no point in going all the way back to the Incident Room now. Not when I've come out this far. And this boy, whoever he is, will still be there when we get to him, hoping and hoping he's got away with it. He won't, though. He won't.

But don't leave it any longer than I have to, putting everything in hand. Still, won't radio in. I'll get this going myself. Hands-on. Make amends for the way I messed up the briefing. This time I'll really have that steamroller determination. Be as hard as it takes.

He started the car, pushed his way through the fog, even thicker on the outskirts of the town, until he reached the cottage in Frogs Lane where Vicky lived with her sports-mad lover. There were lights on in the living-room window and the uncurtained kitchen. So Conor had been getting himself his tea. Surprise, surprise. And now, no doubt, was getting down to his homework. Every Tuesday since this term had begun he had found him doing just that.

But tell Vicky he didn't need supervision? No way.

He almost decided not to bother going in. Be through with the Polworthys all the sooner and back to the Incident Room. But the thought of how not turning up would put Conor on the spot with Vicky when she and Mike came home made him change his mind. The boy had troubles enough without him adding to them.

He tapped hard at the ridiculous tinny goblin door knocker — no, be fair, not necessarily put there by Mike — and in a moment Conor opened up. Short, stocky build, square face with a little jutting knob of a chin, thatch of dark hair, big brown eyes slightly down at the corners. The mirror image of himself at that age, even to the Harrison Academy uniform he, too, had worn in his day. The same badge on the same long black jacket, the same ugly yellow and green striped tie, pulled down from the shirt top button in just the way that had annoyed his own father. Only the scuffed trainers on his feet were different. In his day it had been regulation black shoes, or else . . .

Which reminds me. I'd thought I'd go myself and see the head there about this security-in-schools drive. After all, top school merits a senior officer. Must do it, soon as this investigation's resolved.

'Yo, Dad.'

'Hi.'

And, damn it, at once he was finding it altogether as difficult as usual to say anything that didn't sound patronizing or downright silly.

Conor gave him a grin.

'Yes,' he said. 'I have got myself my tea. I did have enough to eat. Did I wear my cagoule to school? No, I didn't. I never do, unless it's snowing or something. None of us do. And yes, I have begun my homework. Stinking French before I get on with history.'

Stinking French. I do believe I used to call it exactly that too. That god-awful Mr Pasdore who used to take it. About all I remember of what he tried to drum into us: that saying *Tout comprendre c'est tout pardonner.* To understand everything is to forgive everything. Suppose it must have rung a special bell with me, even at that age.

'Well then, your old dad may as well push off.'

'Hey, no, man. I didn't mean it like that. It's only that when Mum rings you up tomorrow, she'll ask all that stuff, and I don't want my *old dad* to have to tell horrible lies.'

Now it was his turn to grin, if more feebly than Conor.

'As a matter of fact,' he said, 'I should push off soon as I can. There's been a murder, and Superintendent Verney's away on a Bramshill course. So I'm in full charge.'

'Right. But what sort of a case is it? Sherlock Holmes stuff, or just some domestic?'

The policeman's son. Ready with the jargon. And, not so good, the job-of-work attitude, a case as something to be *resolved* and nothing more.

'No, it's a bit more than a domestic. An old man living all on his own in a big house down in Sandymount. May turn out to be nothing more than a mugging that went wrong, but we'll see.'

'Sandymount? When was it then?'

'The body wasn't discovered till this morning, but it looks as though the actual murder happened at about six o'clock yesterday evening.'

'But I was there, or —'

He came to an abrupt halt.

'You were down in Sandymount then? What were you doing there? I thought you were meant to come straight home after school.'

Conor looked uncomfortable. But he answered quickly enough.

'Who's nagging now? And, as a matter of fact, Mum isn't quite so hot on me getting straight back from school as she'd like you to think. So, really, Tuesdays are often the only time I do come straight home.'

Home, he thought, with a sudden retch of bitterness. So this is what Conor now thinks of as home. After all the years.

He decided abruptly that he would go on in. Talk to the boy. His son. If only for a minute or two.

In the sitting-room — crammed with fat chintzy armchairs, worn-looking oriental flowered carpet covering only part of the oak-boarded floor, big fireplace with a chunky stone mantelpiece, squitty little electric fire in the hearth — he saw that an exercise book on the gateleg table had a page half filled in, with Conor's French grammar and dictionary open beside the telephone.

And, next to that, there was a spiralbound pad of the sort they had always had for taking messages beside the phone at home. It was, he saw, carefully turned to the newest blank sheet. In just the way theirs had always been kept, ready to use. He felt an odd jab of pleasure. So Vicky's taken with her some of our set routines. I'm not totally cast off, then.

'See your mother's still taking phone messages the old way,' he said, unable to stop himself.

'What? Oh, the pad. Well, I suppose that's more me than Mum. You know what she was always like, tearing out the pages for shopping lists and losing some vital message. Mike's even worse.'

Disappointment. Or not. Better to have put the idea of the message-pad system in your son's head than your wife's? Nearly ex-wife's.

But change the subject. Dangerous waters.

'Well then, what do you do, the days you skive off coming back straight after school?'

'Oh, I dunno. Have a Coke somewhere. Talk with my mates. Mess about. Depends.'

'Any treasure hunting? That what you go down to Sandymount for?'

'Treasure hunting? Oh, God, Dad, call it by its name. I'm a detectorist.'

'Yeah, sorry. Didn't mean to knock it. I'm delighted you've got a worthwhile hobby, in fact.'

And immediately he thought: God, *worthwhile*, what do I sound like? And then he made matters yet worse.

'And how about that girl you're friendly

with? Belinda? She one of the mates you see?'

'Well, I can hardly help seeing her, can I? We are in the same class at school.'

The sulky answer. And a hint, surely, that love's young dream may be taking a wrong turning. Some rival butting in?

And me losing what rapport we had. So what can I say now? Steer clear of Miss Belinda, for one thing. Though not altogether sorry if that's coming to an end. Didn't much like her, times I met her. Snobby little bitch. Dad, that smart dentist. Though suppose she can't really be expected to throw off all her poncy upbringing.

Then, to end the developing awkward silence, he simply plunged.

'Look, lad, I don't want to preach, but —'

'Oh, Dad, come on. "I don't want to preach". Why are you always so bloody understanding? You do want to preach really, don't you? Well, go on, preach. Preach away, I can take it.'

He grinned back, perhaps less feebly than before.

'You win. And anyhow, you know what I was going to say, don't you? A levels at the end of next year, and you could get to university, you know. You've got the brains, and you've got the push. Your keenness on archaeology, metal detecting, all that.'

For a moment then there flashed into his head fat Mrs Damberry's talk about the Hampton Hoard. Should he ask Conor about that? But no. A false lead if ever there was one.

He searched about for something more to say on the subject of schoolwork, something that wouldn't show too much *understanding*.

'Look, you've just got to stick at it this year and next, and you'll find yourself with good enough grades to get into Cambridge or Oxford. Reading archaeology. You could, you know. Start of a great career. PhD, lectureship, professor, startling discovery somewhere, Nobel Prize, if there is a —'

He came to a dead stop.

Nobel Prize. Unwala. That's why I know the name. Poor dead little monkey Mr Unwala in fact none other than Professor Unwala, Nobel Prize winner back in the forties. Physiology, or something. Eventually retired to King's Hampton, with, yes, his English wife, a King's Hampton girl. Big piece in the *Advertiser* at the time. Remember it from years ago. Professor Edul Unwala, the forename's even come back to me. But, oh Christ, this is going to put a whole different complexion on the case. Bloody nationals will want a story, TV, the lot. Not every day a Nobel Prize winner gets murdered. And, yeah, well . . . Well, very likely won't be seen as a case for a mere DCI any longer. Better get on to Headquarters pronto. The Chief will want to know.

'Hey, Dad, what's up? You look as if you've suddenly been hit over the head. You all right?'

'Yes. Yes. But, you see, all of a sudden. I've realized my murder's a top-brass affair. The victim's famous. He won a Nobel Prize. It was years ago, in nineteen forty-five, nineteen forty-six, way back then. Some discovery about the human brain. Hey, yes, the mice. That's what they must be about.'

Conor looked at him.

'You gone off your rocker, Dad? Mice? What mice?'

He managed a laugh.

'Sorry. Mind was racing away. No, you see, in the room where it happened there were cages and cages of mice, each one numbered. I couldn't think before what he wanted with them, but now I see. They must be his specimens. And there was scientific apparatus in two of the bedrooms. I thought it was for some sort of a hobby. But no. No, Professor Unwala must still have been performing experiments. God, that makes it all the sadder somehow.'

'Yes. Yes, it does.'

He saw the look of sudden thoughtfulness on Conor's face, and was glad of it.

'But, look,' he said, 'I really will have to go now. I've got to radio this in, or I'll certainly lose charge of the case.'

'Jeez, Dad, I'm sorry.'

Someone else capable of *understanding*. My son.

He felt an uprush of warm feeling that all but brought tears to his eyes.

Chapter Five

Only after he had radioed to Headquarters did it come to him that, in the excitement of making his discovery, he had never asked Conor what had taken him to disreputable Sandymount. The boy, of course, knew the area because the estuary dunes were the best place locally for using a metal detector, if hardly in the same class as the detectorist camp in Norfolk where he had spent a prized fortnight last summer. But he could not have been treasure hunting — no, forbidden to call it that — on a dark November evening.

So why was he down there? Well, time enough to sort that out when I see him next Tuesday.

The Polworthys' house, he found, was one in a short terrace some speculative builder had contrived to put up almost in the country at the far end of Frogs Lane. Mr Polworthy, in his sixties, heavy in body, long fat face not shaved that day, led him in silence into a rigorously neat sitting room. And went straight back to sit in what was plainly 'his' chair on one side of the tiled fireplace, making no attempt to switch off the television tranquilly pumping out the day's episode in the farm life of *Emmerdale*. A sullen pudding.

His wife, dead Mrs Unwala's sister, sparse, pinched of mouth, silver-gray curls dragooned into place, had not left her upright armchair opposite when he came in. She did take her eyes from the screen to glance at him through pallid-rimmed spectacles, but her fingers stayed fiercely knitting at what looked like a steely grey cardigan.

'I'm afraid I'm the bringer of bad news,' he said.

He waited for a response. It somehow seemed indecent to tell them about the death of their relative by marriage with the drone of country voices issuing remorselessly from the TV and the self-absorbed click-clicking of Mrs Polworthy's knitting needles going steadily on.

Well, perhaps she's simply deadly shy, he thought. You get people like that, almost totally incapable of initiating any conversation. So break it gently.

'It — it's your brother-in-law, Mrs Polworthy,' he said, raising his voice above *Em-*

69

merdale's grumbling.

'Him,' Mr Polworthy barked, eyes still steadily attached to the events on the screen. 'Can't say I hold with him. Never have.'

Jesus, how can anyone come out with a remark like that at the very mention of poor old Professor Unwala. And it's not making my task any easier.

But try again.

'The fact is that early this morning Mr Unwala was found dead.'

From Mr Polworthy simply a grunt. From Mrs Polworthy a quick glance of suspicion from behind the pale-rimmed glasses.

'Well, he's gone then,' she said. 'I suppose it was to be expected. He must be getting on for ninety, you know. Dolly was much the younger, not so old as I am even. Of course, he didn't really look his age. Indians don't.'

All right, neither of them going to be too upset when I tell them the poor old fellow was murdered.

'I'm afraid it wasn't old age Mr Unwala died of. I'm sorry to have to tell you he was murdered, attacked in his house and left dead or dying.'

An expression of pointed indignation did appear now on Mrs Polworthy's taut-checked face. But it might have been produced by the way she had been told the news. Or as a comment on the state of society in general. Certainly there had come no signs of real grief or horror.

'Well,' she said at last, 'I can't say we ever knew him all that well. Dolly met him when she was at Cambridge University. Always was the clever one of the family was Dolly. And much good it did her. Marrying someone from there.'

'From there? From Cambridge?'

'An Indian. She knew nothing about him, you know. Nothing about what they're like.'

'But he was a very distinguished man, wasn't he? A Nobel Prize winner.'

'That's as may be. I'm not saying they're not clever. But they're not like us. I don't know what Dolly meant bringing him back here like that.'

Still not invited to take the third chair round the TV in the scrupulously neat little room, he thought it was probably as well for Professor Unwala that his wife's sister used to see little of them. A dismal cloud of disapproval would have come in with her the moment she stepped into the house. But, see her side of it. Mrs Unwala, her younger sister, and plainly much more intelligent. Top of the class at school here no doubt, then a scholarship to Cambridge. No

71

wonder Mrs Polworthy regarded her with such unyielding sourness, however much she should not.

'I suppose you don't happen to know . . .' Mr Polworthy began solemnly from the other side of the spluttering little fire in the narrow tiled fireplace. Then he came to a halt.

Had his attention been abruptly riveted by some new development in *Emmerdale*? But, no. His eyes were turned towards himself in lugubrious, silent questioning.

'I'm sorry? Do I happen to know what?'

'If there's a will. By rights, Milly here ought to come into the money. There wasn't no one else.'

'But didn't Mr Unwala have relations in India?'

'That he did not,' Mrs Polworthy broke in. 'Many a time Dolly told me he was all alone in the world. I expect that's what made her interested in the first place. She was always like that. Stray dogs, if Mother had ever let her keep them. A blackbird once, with a broken wing. Nasty dirty thing.'

Plainly they don't know if they're going to get any money or not. One possible motive, very doubtful at best, out of the way.

'So you neither of you saw very much of the Unwalas?' he asked, well knowing the answer.

But get as much as possible out of the two of them. If Mrs Ahmed's 'boy' and his mates turn out to be a no-no, we'll need every scrap of background we can get hold of. And that's another thing. Must send over to the *Advertiser*, get a copy of that piece they did, *Nobel Prize Man Comes to King's Hampton*.

'We kept ourselves to ourselves,' Mrs Polworthy answered his question with a little prim nod of her fixed grey curls.

'I didn't hold with 'em, that's all,' Mr Polworthy chimed in.

'But you visited your sister occasionally, didn't you, Mrs Polworthy?'

'How do you know that?'

Her voice cut with sharp suspicion through *Emmerdale*'s exchanges.

'I've been speaking to the lady who came in to look after your brother-in-law, a Mrs Damberry.'

Pursed lips tightened in sourness. Not a word said.

'And did you go on visiting after your sister died?' he went on.

'Certainly not. It was none of my business to interfere.'

'To interfere? Interfere with what, Mrs Polworthy?'

'With anything. With — with those dirty mice of his.'

'Ah, yes. We noted he had a number of mice, I suppose for some research he was still carrying out? Do you know what it was into?'

'I'm sure I don't.'

'You've no idea? Your sister never mentioned anything?'

'She may have done.'

'So what was it? Do you remember at all?'

'Something to do with — with that disease. The one that happens to old people.'

'No sign of that with you, Milly love.'

Mr Polworthy came away from the TV to give a dull chuckle.

'I should hope not.'

'Is that Alzheimer's disease? Was Professor Unwala working on Alzheimer's disease?'

'He may have been. I don't suppose he was getting anywhere with it.'

'Well, he was a brilliant man.'

A sniff.

For a moment he allowed his mind to wander. That little curled-up, tranquil body. The brain that had driven it onwards blotted into nothingness in that smashed head. And the research he was doing . . . Very likely he had still been carrying on with his work on Alzheimer's. That sort of research took time. Years and years of patient experimenting, especially without a university laboratory at his disposal. Just that scanty apparatus, those numbered cages of white mice. The one that escaped once. Not the best of conditions. Yet there he was, little Professor Unwala, steadily working away. *Always reading and reading in those big books of he,* hadn't Mrs Damberry said? And one day he might have made a discovery that would show how that inevitable deterioration could be prevented. And now all of it lost? Very probably, almost certainly. A waste, an utter waste.

And coming out here more waste, come to that. Waste of my time. All right, they had to be told, the pair of them, that her brother-in-law has been murdered. But now they have been. And precious little interest they've shown. Nor have I got anything much out of them. And never likely to, either.

So, home James. Home to where I ought to be: in the Incident Room at least while I'm still in charge of things, putting the fire into the inquiry that I failed to before. And with something substantial now to do it with. The firmly established fact of Mrs Ahmed's *boy* and perhaps a handful of his nasty friends.

Tersely he said he would trouble them no longer, and made his way out. Neither of them left their chair to see him to the door.

And yet, outside, the cold coils of the fog wrapping round him once more, he stood and admitted to himself that they probably lived good enough lives. They did no one any harm. Not for them places in the records in the station basement. Where there were stored the names of dozens of youths 'known to the police'. Among them, with any luck, that of the killer.

'Thank God you're back,' Jumbo Hastings said.

'Why? What's up? What is it?'

Jumbo grinned.

'What's up is I'm dying for a pee, and the paperwork's been piling up.'

'OK, Jumbo. Piss off then, as they say.'

Jumbo heaved himself to his feet and headed, rapidly as his solid legs would take him, in the direction of the toilets. But, at the door, he called back over his shoulder.

'Oh, yes. Forgot. Message for you. Fothergill. He's coming down from HQ. Doesn't say why.'

But he knew why Detective Chief Superintendent Fothergill, whizz-kid head of the Serious Crimes Squad at County Headquarters, known throughout the force as the Gill, was coming from Barminster quickly as his smart BMW would take him. Because little Mr Unwala had turned out to be Nobel Prize winner Professor Unwala. And the eyes of the world, or at least a good handful of TV cameras, would before long be firmly fixed on Barshire County Constabulary.

He had scarcely had time to order the lists of the district's 'bad lads' to be brought up on the computer screens and to arrange with Jumbo, much relieved, for a daylight search of the verge of Seabray Way when the Muster Room door flew open and Fothergill himself came in, already peeling off camel-coloured British Warm to reveal a dark grey pinstriped suit beneath. A narrow predator's face, with a little reddish moustache above a tight compressed mouth. A bristling head of hair of the same pale red as the moustache. Light green eyes darting.

'Right, Mr Benholme, word with you. In your office, if you please.'

'Yes, sir.'

Big stuff. Secret stuff.

Oh, well, the Gill must be allowed his

little ways. Had earned them, actually. Admin skills and brown-nosing get you only so far, and the Gill had got a lot further than that. Plenty of real successes under his belt.

Not allowing him time even to offer the chair behind his desk, or to take it himself, the Gill snapped out what he wanted.

'First of all, I'm leaving you in charge of the Incident Room. But note, please, I want copied to me every scrap of paper that comes in. I'll use your office, and I'll be here all but twenty-four hours a day. Until either the case is resolved or Superintendent Verney comes back from Bramshill. Right?'

'Right, sir.'

'Now then, put me in the picture. The whole picture from start to finish. And be brief. I don't want to be sitting here listening to you at midnight.'

'No, sir.'

He did his best to lay out chronologically everything that had happened. The PC's *Fatal* radio message, his own decision that this was not an accident but murder — No trouble in omitting March's part in that — on to realizing the victim was Nobel Prize-winning Professor Unwala and what he had learnt in his interview with Mrs Ahmed.

'You're certain you can rely on this

woman's evidence? She'll stand up in court?'

'Yes, sir. I questioned her at some length, and she gave me no cause to believe she wasn't thoroughly reliable.'

'Good. Looks as though we might get this dealt with, even before we have to go before the TV cameras. We're in a high-profile situation here, remember, and I don't want mistakes made. Right, now I'll find your list of local bad lads on your computer here?'

'It won't be up just yet, sir. I'd only just come back from seeing the deceased's next of kin when you arrived.'

'But you'd had this Mrs Ahmed's evidence before you went out to these people?'

'Yes, sir.'

'Then I suggest if you continue to have a part in this inquiry you do not leave reporting in important information until you take it into your head that it's convenient. Damn it, man, you're not a wooden-top filling in forms on house-to-house. You're a detective. Try to act like one.'

'Yes, sir. I'm sorry, sir.'

Only thing to do, eat humble pie. But he needn't have made such a performance of it, just to show what a bloody hard-nosed high-flyer he is. A word would have been enough.

As I hope I use when I have to rebuke

someone not entirely incompetent.

'And these next of kin, did you do anything more when you saw them than sit there offering condolences?'

Tempting to say I didn't even get to sit. But humour him, humour him.

'Yes, sir, I did. I found out there's no other relatives, either here or in India. And I ascertained the pair of them had only the vaguest hopes of benefiting under any will.'

He decided in an instant not to say anything about discovering that Professor Unwala had been working on Alzheimer's. It wasn't particularly relevant, and somehow he didn't like the thought of the Gill trampling with his little sharp feet over more than was strictly necessary of the old man's life.

'All right. Well, see that list of youths gets up on my screen. And as soon as maybe.'

'Yes, sir.'

With relief he left.

But no sooner had he got back to the Incident Room than a message came in from one of the constables still plodding round in the cold and fog on catch-up house-to-house inquiries. Mr Harold Jones, an elderly asthmatic, had been at the hospital all day until this evening. But twenty-four hours earlier he had been sitting at his open window at number four Percival Road trying, despite the fog, to ease his lungs with some fresh air. And over a period of a quarter of an hour or more he had seen a man in 'a black coat' standing about at the far end of the road at a time shortly before six P.M. He was certain about the hour because he had hoped his asthma would have subsided before the six o'clock news. But, too concerned about his condition to have paid the lurker much attention, he could provide no more information. All he was sure about was the black coat.

Could this be one of the gang of yobbos? Left back to keep a lookout? The time was certainly about right. Pity the description was so bad, but there had been the fog and by then it would have been dark. Still, this was another pointer.

He beckoned to one of the cadets on duty.

'Take this to Detective Chief Superintendent Fothergill, lad. You'll find him in my office.'

The cadet took the copy message.

'And, lad.'

'Sir?'

'Smarten yourself up a bit, and mind your p's and q's when you speak to Mr Fothergill. Right?'

The message brought the Gill himself into

the Incident Room almost at a run.

'This is the sort of break I'd hoped for, Mr Benholme. A black coat. Do you see the significance of that?'

He didn't. Only thing, say so.

'Not sure that I do, sir.'

'No? Well, think what's our most prevalent policing problem just now.'

Bloody riddles. This the way the Gill got his reputation for being bright? Well, no. He is bright.

'You tell me, sir.'

'Britforce, Chief Inspector. Britforce, a major national semi-Fascist organization with its heart in Barshire and its so-called troopers parading about all over the county. I'm surprised you didn't come up with Britforce the moment you set eyes on this message. Britforce thugs in their trademark black mace.'

Should he have thought of them as soon as he had read about that black coat? But the description hadn't in fact put any immediate picture of a black-mackintoshed Britforce trooper on guard outside Professor Unwala's while some racist thuggery took place. Perhaps it ought to have done. Hadn't Bob Carter only this morning talked about *black-mac stirrers?*

'Well, yes, sir, true enough. Britforce

thugs are a problem in the town here at times. More, I suppose, for you in Barminster, but they make trouble in King's Hampton too.'

'Right then, you can forget about the local riff-raff now. I want you to concentrate full out on Britforce. Go yourself to their HQ first thing tomorrow. Question that fellow Marcus Pennings who runs the outfit. Find out where every one of his troopers was at the time of the killing. Every single one. Have a word with Inspector Travis at Special Branch first. And take — who is it? — DI Carter with you. I want this treated as absolute top priority.'

'Excuse me, sir. But with Mr Verney away, we've no senior detective to hold the fort here bar Mr Carter.'

'I can't help that. You should be better organized. You never know when an emergency might occur. Make some other arrangement. If anything really serious comes up I shall be here. I'm perfectly capable of dealing with two cases at once. But I want two senior officers to tackle Pennings. Understood?'

'Yes, sir.'

Chapter Six

Professor Unwala roughed up fatally by
Britforce troopers? Thugs who happened to
be passing when by chance — another
mouse escaping? — the old man had opened
his front door? It wouldn't, he thought, be
the first time Britforce bully boys had beaten
up a black in King's Hampton. So it all
certainly seemed to fit in. That *u-rine-ated*
incident a month ago, the *black bastard* yell,
the lurking man in the black mackintosh, if
that was what asthmatic Mr Jones had
meant by 'black coat'.

But then there was Mrs Ahmed's cast-iron
certainty about that yell. That it had come
from a boy. A Britforce trooper that young?
Well, perhaps it was possible, just. If only
just.

However, Detective Chief Superintendent
Fothergill was convinced. And had issued
his orders.

So do what I'm told. Phone Inspector
Travis at Special Branch. See what he has

to say about youngsters as Britforce troopers. He ought to know whether there were any. After all, Britforce must be almost the only subversive outfit in the area.

'Britforce?' came the snapped-out answer from County Headquarters. 'There isn't much I don't know about that organization.'

'Just what I want to hear, Inspector. The truth is I detest the whole thought of all that sort of thing, and I'm afraid I've blocked it from my mind up to now.'

'Mistake there, I think, Mr Benholme. If things go the way those people want, as they well may, then you could find before long that Britforce is playing a very considerable part in your life.'

Was there a hint of acceptance in his voice? A police disciplinarian responding to similar sentiments coming at him from, as it were, the other direction?

Better go a bit carefully.

'Well, what it is: I'm afraid Britforce is going to be playing more of a part in my life tomorrow morning than I altogether welcome. DCS Fothergill's sending me to interview that man Marcus Pennings about the possible involvement of Britforce troopers in the murder we've had here in King's Hampton.'

'Oh, yes. The buzz round here is the vic-

85

tim's some sort of Nobel Prize winner. Is that right?'

News travels fast. Barshire Police Headquarters a hotbed of gossip. Still, it'll be all over the media soon enough.

'Yes, Inspector, that's what he is. Was. Nobel Prize for Physiology, some time in the nineteen forties. So you can see we want a quick result.'

'Then what can I tell you, in particular?'

'Well, put me more in the picture about Marcus Pennings for a start.'

'Right. Well, I'd advise you to tread very carefully with him. He doesn't tolerate opposition. Of any sort. Police, left-wingers, anybody. If he doesn't like anything you say, he'll be on to the Chief Constable before your back's turned. And he'll take your words out of context. He fights dirty, Marcus Pennings. He's tough, too. You won't be able to bully anything out of that one.'

'I see. So I'll have to be a bit cunning? Soft-soap approach?'

'I doubt if that'll do you much good. He'll see through it in less time than it takes to tell. And he'll cut up all the rougher.'

'A real hard nut then.'

'That's him.'

'Well, I'll have to manage best as I can.

Still, thanks for the warning. But there's one other thing.'

'Yes?'

'About the uniform Britforce troopers wear. Aren't I right that in fact the wearing of uniform by civilians is banned? Has been right from the time of the pre-war Fascists?'

'Yes. That's the strict interpretation of the law. But we can't enforce it too rigorously these days. It's convenient, for instance, for security firms to give their personnel a distinctive look.'

'I suppose so. So about the Britforce uniform, or semi-uniform. We've a report of an individual in a black coat seen hanging about near the murder scene. What chance would there be of identifying him as Britforce?'

'A black coat? Well, that might be anything. I've got a topcoat myself that's pretty dark. But, yes, if your witness can say the fellow was wearing a long black mackintosh, then you could make a reasoned guess he's Britforce. Though on the other hand there's no law against black macs. Anyone can have one.'

'So we're going to have to let that one go?'

'I'd say you are. Well, anything else I can tell you?'

'Yes, just one thing. Does Britforce take on boys?'

'Boys? What d'you mean *boys*?'

'Just that really. Boys young enough to have voices still at least occasionally going treble.'

'Well, can't say I've seen much sign of them taking anyone on young as that. Certainly weren't any kids that age at that rally of theirs down your way. Commemoration of the famous Battle of King's Hampton, last foreign force to be thrown back from British shores. Only that was just a couple of dozen shipwreck survivors, what I hear.'

'Yes, seem to remember being told that at school here. Still, we live in the age of hype. Mustn't forget that.'

And do I have anything more to ask? No, don't think so. Heard more than I really want to, especially about Marcus Pennings. A nasty customer.

Ah, well.

'No, I think that's all, Inspector. Thanks for your help.'

So, with Bob Carter sitting beside him, he drew up at a few minutes past nine next morning in front of a small shop in a Barminster backstreet. A pair of crossed black flags with the Britforce clenched-fist emblem on them displayed in the dusty window told him he had found the right place. Also, according to Inspector Travis, the home of Marcus Pennings.

'Right then, Bob. I don't need to tell you: we'll have to go bloody carefully here.'

'I don't see why. Christ, if those sodding neo-Fascists, whatever they are, have done in someone on our patch, black or white, I can't see why we shouldn't go for them hell for leather. What they need is to be taught a bloody good lesson.'

'I dare say,' he answered. 'But the fact is, if we've got it wrong about Britforce thugs being our chummies, Marcus Pennings is the sort of person capable of raising a very nasty stink.'

'But we aren't wrong, are we? Bloody Fothergill sending senior officers mob-handed. Must mean something.'

'OK. But remember, even the Gill can make a mistake. Sometimes.'

'Suppose so. Can't say I'd mind if this turned out to be one of the times. Bloody I'm-going-to-be-a-Chief, so you look out.'

'Well, we'll see.'

He got out, went over, tried the shop door and when that proved locked, rang long and hard at the bell beside it.

The heavily built man who answered, after a long enough wait, was everything that he had thought a Britforce thug would be. Hair cropped almost to shadow point, grey shirt buttoned at the neck with matching trousers that might or might not be a uniform, he stared out at them with a look of sullen aggression on his heavily moustached, dark-complexioned face.

'Yes?' he said.

'We're police officers.' He pulled out his warrant card. 'We want to see Mr Marcus Pennings.'

'You can't.'

'No question of can't about it. We're here to interview him. Is he in the house or not?'

'He's in. But he doesn't have no truck with police.'

The thug, or trooper, stood there fisted hands on hips, defiant.

He sighed. Hard to understand a brute like this. Suppose he may have had a wretched upbringing of some sort. But, if this is a specimen of Marcus Pennings's army, what's the man himself going to be like?

'We want no trouble,' he said. 'But I'm warning you: unless you let us in to see Mr Pennings we'll have you, and him, in a cell before you know what's hit you.'

He looked the trooper in the eye, unwaveringly.

And won.

'OK then, if you must.'

Soft as a duck's arse, he thought to himself with an access of cheerfulness as, followed by Bob Carter, he made his way into the shop.

More clenched-fist flags, a row of bright paperback books with titles like *Britain for the British, Britain First and Britain Best* and *The Battle of King's Hampton* displayed on a shelf behind the pamphlet-piled counter. Weapons, he wondered. No guns, of course. But bludgeons for sale? But there was nothing he could see.

The thug led them into a back kitchen where the man he supposed must be Marcus Pennings was sitting at the plastic-covered table watching a boy of about ten eating a bowl of cornflakes.

'Good morning,' he said. 'Is it Mr Pennings? Marcus Pennings?'

'It is. And who are you?'

Marcus Pennings, as he rose from his chair, could be seen to be almost as well built as his thuggish trooper, wearing the same grey shirt and semi-uniform. But his face, by contrast, was open and even seemed welcoming under its equally close-cropped

91

hair, blond rather than muddy dark.

Once more he produced his warrant card, introducing this time Bob Carter.

Pennings held out his hand for the card, looked at it with care and handed it back. With a curt 'Leave us', he dismissed his trooper. Then he turned to the boy at the table.

'Gobble that up, Tom,' he said, giving him a friendly tap on the top of his blond head. 'You'll have to go now.'

He turned to Benholme.

'If you'll excuse me, I'll just get this boy of mine off to school. Late, of course. But, seeing that all they teach them there is a lot of liberal whitewash, I don't see it much matters.'

A remark best not pursued.

To be expected, of course, from the Britforce commander. But the way he had behaved with his son, now scuttling cheerfully out in front of him, was not exactly how one might have thought a martinet would act. And where was the wife? Dead? Divorced? Run away? Travis had said nothing about any wife, or wife trouble. But whatever, Pennings was apparently left looking after his son.

Unlike Phil Benholme, he thought wryly.

Through the door Pennings had left open

behind him he heard 'Eat your lunch', and 'Tell your teacher I said you could be late'. Then Pennings came back in.

'Well, gentlemen,' he said, 'what brings you here bright and early in the morning?'

Despite his apparent friendliness, he answered him as stiffly as he could.

'We're inquiring into the death on Monday evening of a Mr Unwala who lived in the Sandymount area of King's Hampton. Do you know it?'

'Do I know King's Hampton? Of course I do. The site of the battle where the only real invasion of England was beaten back.'

Another remark to be ignored.

'I meant do you know the Sandymount area?'

'Ah, I'm sorry. I'm afraid the very mention of King's Hampton is inclined to carry me away.'

But, smooth though that was, it was no answer to the question.

'Sandymount, sir?'

'Oh, yes. Yes, of course, Sandymount. No, Chief Inspector, I can't say I do know that particular area of King's Hampton. It wasn't where the battle took place, you know.'

'Yes, sir. I do know that, as a matter of fact.'

He was glad of the opportunity to deliver that much of a rebuke. No harm in seeing what response it got. The tiger's claws.

But they were still sheathed.

'I'm glad to hear you know that much of your country's history, Chief Inspector.'

'Every police officer from King's Hampton is likely to know about that "battle", sir. Thanks to your organization.'

Despite the slight mocking emphasis he had put on *battle*, Marcus Pennings again seemed totally unruffled. But now the subject of Britforce and its thugs had been brought to the fore.

'In fact, it's the presence of Britforce personnel in King's Hampton on Monday night, specifically in the Sandymount area, that we want to talk to you about, sir.'

No sign of discomposure. But perhaps Marcus Pennings had not heard what that party of his troopers had done. On the other hand, if everything Travis had said about the man was correct, he enforced strict discipline in his organization. So a beating-up that had ended as a fatality should have been reported to him.

'The presence of Britforce members in Sandymount on Monday evening, Chief Inspector? Can you tell me what sort of time you're talking about? I can't be responsible for the actions of the volunteers who make up Britforce all of the time. They have their own lives to live, you know.'

Can't be responsible . . . all of the time. Are we beginning to get somewhere now? The evasive excuse?

But Bob Carter, kept out of things too long, chose this moment to come bouncing in.

'Six P.M. on Monday night,' he snapped, plainly hoping to extract some admission.

Damn the fellow.

But what if he pulls it off?

Pennings smiled.

'Monday at six, Inspector? Well, you should know where my troopers were then.'

Carter frowned.

'And why is that?'

'Because we were all at our battle anniversary rally in King's Hampton Town Hall, observed by Inspector Travis of Special Branch and by one of your own local plain-clothes officers. That very handsome red-haired Detective Sergeant March, there to see we kept good order and discipline. Which we did. I made sure of that.'

Jesus, but yes, of course. Bob had even mentioned that March was there yesterday when she made that loud-voiced *soft as a duck's arse* remark. He should have bloody well realized the rally was already taking place at six o'clock. I didn't know it was as early as that, but he should have done. If he read March's report already on his desk then. And here's Pennings apparently claiming all his thugs were safely inside the Town Hall at the time.

'Excuse me, sir, but are you saying all your — your troopers were at that rally in King's Hampton Town Hall?'

'I most certainly am, Chief Inspector. I wouldn't like to be one of my men who'd failed to report for duty on the night of the Battle of King's Hampton. In fact, I called the roll myself. Hundred per cent attendance.'

But make it all crystal clear.

'May I get this quite straight? All your troopers, every one of them, from all over the county, were at the King's Hampton rally at six P.M. on Monday?'

'Yes, Chief Inspector. I would have allowed anyone seriously ill to be off duty, but there was no one. We're a pretty fit force, you know.'

'And the rally began when?'

'At five P.M. promptly.'

'And finished when?'

'At eight. We were not allowed the use of the hall after that. A piece of petty bureaucratic interference. Which is why we had to begin so early. And why we were prevented from marching through the town.'

Now the claws were showing. Would they strike at any moment?

But I'm not going to be intimidated, though Bob looks as if he's no longer as ready for the fray as he was before we came in. But I'm going to get at the full truth of this. The facts are crucial.

'Let me get this absolutely right, Mr Pennings. All your troopers were there in the hall the whole time? None of them left for any reason?'

'Once again, Chief Inspector, I wouldn't like to have been in the shoes of anyone who'd dared. I think you'll find that confirmed in any report your Detective Sergeant March may have made.'

No doubt we will. The cocky bastard.

But, once more, don't let him off the hook just on his own say-so. And I think I may have something that will upset this calm of his. Yes, I believe I may.

'I'm sorry to persist with my inquiries,' he said. 'But we have certain information that points towards brutal behaviour from Britforce personnel at that time, brutal behaviour that may have resulted in murder.'

He was just aware of Bob Carter beside him showing signs of uneasiness. But he knew much less of the business.

'Brutal behaviour? Chief Inspector, you had better be very careful about what you're saying. You have my word that not one of my men was at large in King's Hampton at the time you tell me this murder took place. Challenge that if you will. But I warn you: I am more than happy to have recourse to the full weight of the law if you prove to be wrong.'

Bob was now rigid as a bar of ice just at his back.

'I take note of what you have said, sir. But what I must ask you now is: have any of your troopers ever in the past gone into a house in the Sandymount area of King's Hampton for the purpose of terrorizing a gentleman of Indian origin who lived there?'

A gamble. A hell of a gamble. Nothing fat Mrs Damberry had said in telling him of the *u-rine-ated* incident had really indicated that Britforce troopers were responsible. It could, in fact, be down to any bunch of racist yobbos. But, on the other hand, the attack had all the marks of more organized brutality than casual passing yobs might rise to.

And in Marcus Pennings's handsome face he saw his answer. A tiny eye-flicker of pierced confidence.

'Some four weeks ago, sir?' he pressed on. 'Was that incident then not reported to you? Or was it?'

'Yes, Chief Inspector. Yes, it was, as a matter of fact. I pride myself on keeping my whole organization under strict control. Sometimes it is necessary to fight fire with fire. Our activities arouse a good deal of opposition among the intruders this country is swamped with. So when we do fight back, we do so as a force under orders. Yes, I did learn of the incident you mention, though I never heard of the name of the man who was, yes again, its victim. You are telling me now that it was actually this Mr — Mr Unwala who has subsequently been murdered?'

'I am.'

Then Marcus Pennings smiled.

'I can see the reasoning that brought you here, Chief Inspector. But it was, if I may say so, just one more example of the prejudice my organization finds in the police. However, leave that aside. I am happy to say that my reaction to that attack on this Mr Unwala goes a long way towards showing that no one from my force had anything to do with the subsequent attack made on him. Apart, that is, from my assurance that all my men were at the time inside King's Hampton Town Hall.'

'And what is that, sir?'

'The simple fact, Chief Inspector, that those responsible on the former occasion were severely punished. Under my direct supervision.'

But now Bob Carter bounced back in.

'Can't believe that just because you say so.'

'No, Inspector. As I was saying, you police officers tend to be somewhat heavily biased against my movement. Perhaps if you were not under orders to harass us, you would have a different point of view. But we won't go into that. What I can do for you, however, is to show you plain evidence of the punishment I had to have inflicted for that incident.'

'Evidence? What sort of evidence?' Bob truculent as ever.

'Evidence on the back of that trooper who brought you in here, Inspector. He was whipped. And when I feel that such punishment is necessary, I see that it's carried out to the full. So do you want to see Trooper Peel's back? Or will you take my word for it?'

Time to jump in, before Bob adds to the complications.

'Very well, Mr Pennings, I am happy to believe that a number of your men assaulted Mr Unwala some four weeks ago, and that one or more of them has been assaulted in his turn. I may add that I don't see charges being brought in this particular case, though I must warn you that we will not always treat such matters as private affairs.'

It was only as they stood in the mean little street outside that another thought struck him. I've got to go back now and tell this to the Gill. Tell him his instant solution doesn't stand up. Check with March, of course, first. And perhaps with Travis. But, little doubt about it, it's me for Detective Chief Superintendent Fothergill and *you've gone and made a bloody fool of yourself, sir*.

The short interview he had, back at his own commandeered office, made the ensuing hour spent in the mortuary in attendance while the County Home Office pathologist carried out his examination of the tiny body of Edul Unwala seem almost a pleasure. The always unnerving sight of the scalpel slicing its way down the length of the sternum and the ribcage being sawn through and forcibly prised open with a chisel was

101

a good deal more endurable than the Gill's response.

He had endeavoured to keep his voice perfectly neutral while he gave him the facts, unembellished.

Then he waited for the explosion.

'Chief Inspector, you are in charge of the CID in King's Hampton. This meeting, or rally as they call it, was taking place within your bailiwick. And you have the effrontery to stand there and tell me that one of your own officers, Detective Sergeant March, was present at it and you still did not realize that it raised considerable doubts over the hypothesis that this murder was the work of Britforce troopers?'

'I hadn't realized that the rally had included every Britforce member, sir.'

'But did it, Chief Inspector? Did it? As far as I can see you have only the word of a notorious fascist for that. What steps did you take to prove or disprove his assertion? You say he offered to show you the back of that man he had had beaten. But did you do it? Did you question him? You did not.'

Then he waited, icily, for a response.

He took a deep breath.

'No, sir. I saw no point in taking up that offer. It was made in a spirit of sheer bravado. Marcus Pennings wanted me to see what sort of a hard man he was. And I wasn't going to give him the pleasure.'

'That's no excuse, Chief Inspector. No excuse acceptable to me. Evidence, evidence of a sort, was put before you and you failed to examine it.'

'Yes, sir. In fact, I saw no necessity for that. I had only to put myself in Pennings's shoes. He was not going to offer what he did if he couldn't have produced this Trooper Peel knowing the fellow would substantiate his statement.'

'Well, I hope your confidence in Marcus Pennings turns out to be justified, Chief Inspector. But, let me tell you now, it is confidence I do not share.'

Back in the Incident Room he realized at once that, however much the Gill's famous hypothesis about Britforce was now looking dodgy, the man's presence had produced that air of lively determination that he himself had failed to generate at his first briefing.

Well, he's done it. Grant him that. Never mind that his theory was inspired, I bet, as much by a desire to tackle a nation-sized bogeyman as by the facts, the room now is buzzing with eagerness to get a result. Not that it's so far produced anything worth getting excited about. Sod all, really, from the post-mortem just now. Confirmation, of course, that poor Professor Unwala did die within an hour either side of six o'clock. Report in from the forensic lab: a considerable amount of whisky in the vomit Jumbo was so pleased to get polished-nails aide Mo Hart to collect. But, though that's interesting enough, there doesn't seem to be anything to deduce from it. Or not until we have someone in the frame.

And nothing so far from the searchers along the tangled verge of Seabray Way. Nothing, too, from the now resumed doorstepping of local 'bad lads'. Most of them out at this time of day, of course.

So sit here, read reports, action anything that looks worth any sort of follow-up. And hope.

At midday there came the press conference the Gill had seen himself triumphing at. And there were quite as many TV cameras whirring away as he had expected, even though he had precious little to say when they were on him. Nothing at all about Britforce. Even if he still hoped that his juicy line of inquiry would eventually pay dividends, clearly he was not going to stick his neck out over it now.

But, he asked himself bitterly as he sat there doing his best to look alert and supportive, who was it who had somehow got into Professor Unwala's house round about six P.M.? Who had struck that single death-dealing blow and hastily attempted to make it look as if it was the result of that bookcase falling over? Who had then — it was almost certain — left by way of the overgrown, neglected garden, scaled the tall fence at the end putting beside it just one footmark? And who possibly had vomited up whisky as he went?

Early in the afternoon one further piece of evidence did come to hand. The search team at the throughway found, thrust into thick grass under one of the tangled bushes on the verge, what looked as if it must be the weapon. It was a cricket bat. A very old bat, its willow seamed with long cracks, the fifties-style orange rubber covering of its handle hopelessly perished. At its end, clearly visible through its plastic evidence bag, was a dark stain.

'A fair bet that it belonged to the old fellow,' Jumbo Hastings said to him. 'They haven't made bats like that since what would have been his cricketing days. Had an old one meself, just like it, when I was a nipper. Funny him being a cricketer, though.'

'No,' he answered. 'I've been reading the files sent over from the *Advertiser*. Professor Unwala was a Parsee, and apparently they're great cricket players. The piece about him coming to the town even mentioned him playing. But what would be a sort of revenge for him, would be if this old bat of his has the killer's prints on it. I'd like that.'

'Know what you mean,' Jumbo said. 'But I very much doubt if Fingerprints'll get anything. That grip's so wrinkled and perished it won't have held a thing, let alone it being out in the fog all night.'

'You're probably right. And in any case, if you think about it, whoever held that bat when he brought it down on the poor old fellow's head would have hardly touched it with his fingertips, not gripping it the way he'd have to.'

But who had gripped it like that? They were no nearer knowing than they had been at the start.

Then, abruptly, a picture came into his mind of a young and agile Edul Unwala playing cricket somewhere — at Cambridge? — and nimbly scuttling from one wicket to the other, scoring run after run.

He must, after all, have been a dab hand at the crease to have treasured his ancient seamed and cracked bat for so many years.

His seamed, cracked and now bloodstained bat.

So the weary hours continued to go by. Reports flopped down in front of him as he sat at the top of the Incident Room. Plastic cups of stewed tea accumulated beside him and half-filled the waste bin under his table. He read. He tried to think if anything he saw added something of value. He scribbled down his initials. Every now and again the Gill came hurricaning in, snapped out some questions, pulled a long face at the answers and disappeared again.

At last there came the final briefing of the day. The Gill, of course, conducted it. All the officers on the inquiry were present, looking for the most part pretty dispirited. The phosphorescent fire the Gill had put into things when he had taken over was almost visibly shrinking away. And his own attempt to rouse some new determination by adding to the Gill's summing-up that the victim had been working on Alzheimer's disease at the time of his death fell even flatter.

'Questions?' the Gill barked at last.

Silence. It began to look as if there would be none at all. But suddenly DS March bounced to her feet, cluster of curls bobbing.

'Not a question, sir,' she said in her characteristically loud tones. 'But I'd just like to point out that if I'd been told what conclusions had been drawn from this report of a black-coated figure loitering near the house I could've pointed out straight off that every man in Britforce was in the Town Hall. I watched Marcus Pennings making a big thing of calling the roll. So, sir, what are we to make of the black-coat sighting now? Has anybody thought of that?'

Cheeky bitch, he thought. I wouldn't dare refer in that way to what was after all the Gill's snatched-at mistake. I wonder if he'll —

And then it came to him. He nearly burst out with it on the spot. There was another group in King's Hampton who wore black coats. Not the long black macs that Britforce paraded about in but, answering equally to asthmatic Mr Jones's description, the black jackets that were Harrison Academy regulation uniform. Jackets which, so Conor had boasted to him last evening, the boys prided themselves on not covering up even in fog-clammy November.

And Conor distinctly evasive, it came back to him now, when he had asked him why he had been in Sandymount on Monday evening. The murder time.

108

Chapter Seven

Oh, come on, he said to himself as he stood there. Come on, you can't really believe Conor had anything to do with it. Why should he have? And, damn it, I know my son. He isn't a murderer. Not possibly.

But then how many murderers are murderers before they commit their crime? A moment of sudden overwhelming rage, and in that instant their lives are changed. From ordinary human being to culpable killer. And which of us isn't capable, given the right circumstances — the wrong, wrong circumstances — of flying into an unstoppable rage?

All right, the worst that such outbursts lead most of us into is no more than a hasty blow. But there are those who, in some particular situation, just don't have the luck to prevent themselves going that one step further. From doing something that results in someone losing their life.

And Conor, could he have found himself

in such a situation? He oughtn't to have done. Yes, he has a temper. But we always checked him when it burst out. Nearly always, surely. Confronted at his present age by something or somebody that fired him with furious rage, he ought to have been able to stop himself lashing out.

But could he? Has he in fact been taught to control himself enough?

No, put it fair and square. Was I too lenient with him? Did I see too easily what the temptations were that faced him? Let him off too lightly? Was I too soft with him? Isn't that what Vicky used to say to me? Often; and often by the time we'd got to the stage of unending rows? And has Conor, caught up in some hard to imagine circumstances, now actually gone that one terrible step too far?

Hard to think how it could have come about. But it might have done. It might, for some as yet inconceivable reason. Conor — who has better reason to know this than me? — is in a fraught state, however little he shows it. But, after fourteen, fifteen years of having his mother and father always there, whatever rows we had and tried to hide, suddenly, almost within the space of a month, to find the two of us propelled apart. To find himself removed to another home. Provided with another father, more or less. Oh, yes, Conor could well be in a state where, when something — What? — happened and he had let fly in fury. Yelled out *You black bastard* — could Conor have ever shouted that? — and then had snatched that ancient cricket bat and struck out.

It could be. In a way it could be. Because wasn't Mrs Ahmed utterly sure the yell had come from a boy with an unbroken voice? And Conor's voice is at the stage when he never knows how it will come out, a hoarse treble or an absurdly man-like bass. So it could have been him. It could.

And then, worse, worse, worse. When he said *Dad, I'm sorry* to me, just as I was leaving the cottage, I thought he was sympathizing with me because I would no longer have the case, now it was such a high-profile affair. I felt such affection for him at that moment. But was that *I'm sorry* said for a wholly different reason? Was he on the point of saying he was sorry the terrible thing he'd done was going to cause me far worse pain? Was he trying to say something like that, and not able to get out more than those two or three words?

Would he ever be able to say more than that? To confess? How can I possibly ever get him to be ready to do that? Me? No, it'll have to be someone else. Another detective. Detective Chief Superintendent Fothergill determined to break the case, to take one more step in his no-holds-barred zoom to the top?

Christ, no. No, I see now, if it's to be done it must be by me. I have to get Conor to tell me what he did before there's any question of it being a police matter. But how? How can I break my own son?

But . . . But do I need to? Do I really need to? Isn't this all just a nightmare construction in my own head? God, I'm beginning to hope now that the Gill's right after all about Britforce. What a burden would suddenly be lifted from me then.

But the thought of a possible Britforce cuffing-up that went wrong led immediately to another. What actual circumstances could have brought, not a young Britforce bully, but Conor into contact with Professor Unwala?

Simple answer. The Hampton Hoard. After all, if Conor's as keen as he is about metal detecting, the prospect of being the one to find the Hampton Hoard . . . And, down in Sandymount regularly combing the dunes, he was bound to have heard the Hoard rumour. And quite likely, too, to have been told that Mrs Unwala before her final illness had actually pinpointed the place. Then . . . Then Conor could well be the person who tried to get the secret out of Professor Unwala. And, yes, had killed him.

I'll have to see him straight away. Now. Find the right questions to ask about what he was doing in Sandymount then. Perhaps, though, he'd only been there for a short while straight after school. All this a terrible false alarm? A ridiculous false alarm.

But see him.

Then he looked at his watch.

Of course, gone half past ten. He'd lost count of time. Conor would be in bed by now. And, under the chair in his room with his clothes placed neatly on it — always neat and tidy, Conor — there would be his trainers. Size seven. Or, at least; I think that's what they are. I think that was his size, at least till recently. Small feet, like mine.

Size seven trainers. And that lifted footprint from the garden.

But no point in waking Conor now. All this may really be no more than some nightmare brought on by tiredness and frustration.

And in any case how could I explain tonight to Vicky, and to her Mike come to that, what I think Conor may have done?

The thought that's come into my head? Vicky would explode. She'd never understand in a million years.

No, sleep on it. And in the morning look at it all calmly once again. Then, if it really does seem there's a chance Conor was in that house and . . . Well, then I can get out to Frogs Lane early, lie in wait for him as he sets off for school and talk to him. In private.

He blinked and looked around. The Gill had left. And so had most of those who had been working on the case, some to pursue inquiries in the town, routing out more bad lads — would one of them strike gold? Remove this nightmare cloud from him? — others to the Recreation Area bar or to their beds.

Might as well go home myself. Someone in shortly to relieve Jumbo, and overnight nothing much likely to happen. Unless I'm woken with a call to say some door-stepped yobbo's made a bolt for it.

If only . . .

Then, as he made his way out, he heard once again March's loud voice. It was coming from round the corridor corner.

'Yes, sir. I'll do that. Go over there first thing. And I promise you I won't let that bastard off the hook so lightly.'

What bastard is this? And who's she talking to? Must be the Gill. But it hardly seems he's bollocking her for what she said at the briefing.

'Good, Sergeant. I wouldn't like you to think the Britforce angle's out of the question. I assure you it isn't. Not by any means.'

Good God. The man's still trying to justify that one impulsive action. And he's enlisted March to help him. Trust him to turn her lack of respect to good account. Well, he's right to this extent: March'll strong-arm her way to seeing that poor devil's bruised and beaten back all right. Hope she gets some pleasure from the sight. Because that's all she will get. Marcus Pennings isn't such a fool as to try to con us with totally fabricated evidence. Not when it could be checked out in a couple of minutes.

No, damn it, I'll back my insight about Pennings against the Gill's grabbed-up view any day.

A night of fitful wakefulness, and tormenting thoughts. And a morning where, he realized as he woke, the fog had at last lifted, though the sky above was dark with ominous clouds.

My fog hasn't lifted though, he thought,

as, rapidly shaved, washed and dressed, he hacked himself a slice of bread, buttered it and gulped a mug of instant coffee, half-warm.

Then, well before Conor was likely to leave to catch his bus for Harrison Academy, he was there, sitting in his car, at the end of Frogs Lane. Ten minutes later Conor came swinging into view, walking briskly along, self-contained, head up, with every appearance of steady cheerfulness. And wearing the long black Harrison Academy jacket, grey regulation trousers, no other protection from the cold, and — what else? — trainers.

Can it be? Can this be a killer coming towards me, however much he may be a killer betrayed by a moment of frustrated rage? My son? My son, the killer. But there's evidence. Enough evidence to make it a prima facie case.

'Conor, hey. I'll drive you to Harrison.'

The boy halted in surprise. And then came up at a half-run.

The guilty party? How can it be? Or are there depths to him, a deep-seated slyness, I've never so much as suspected? Or did the moment when he brought that old cricket bat down on Professor Unwala's white-haired skull do something to him that could never now be changed? Give him a dense and devious protective covering?

No sign of anything different in him, however, as he went round to the passenger side of the car, flicked the door open, slid into the seat.

For some minutes they drove in silence.

Unable to stop himself, he glanced down every few seconds at Conor's feet. Yes, one of those trainers could have left that footmark.

But is seven actually Conor's size? Do I really remember? Should I? A father's duty? Perhaps not.

Ask Conor to hand the trainers over? Send them to Forensic to check against the lifted footmark, examine for tiny traces of earth? But how to do that without alerting him, clamming him up?

No. No, I must do this myself. By putting the trick questions, sliding them in. The trick questions. To my own son.

But before he had found a word to say — why didn't I prepare for this, he snarled at himself — Conor turned to him.

'How's the murder inquiry going, Dad? Did they let you stay in charge?'

Is he just being clever? My son I've always thought so open? Is it now anything to conceal from me what he did there in Sandymount? Or is he even trying to find out how much I, how much the police, know?

'Detective Chief Superintendent Fothergill's running the show,' he answered tersely.

'You've talked about him before, haven't you? Bit of a prick?'

Did I say that? Perhaps I did. But it's not altogether true. The Gill may be a prick, but he's a bloody intelligent one. Ambitious all right, but hard too. No doubt about that. So what will you think, my son, when he has you on the other side of a table in an interview room? He'll slowly split you open till your every last thought lies there for all to see.

'Conor,' he broke out at last, unable now to stop himself, 'what were you doing in Sandymount on Monday?'

'I — I wasn't in Sandymount. Why should I have been?'

'Oh, Conor, no. You were there. You were. You told me so when I came round.'

'No, I didn't.'

The flat denial. Poor lad, is he reduced to that? Christ, I've only to hammer away for a bit, way I would with any ordinary suspect, and he'll spill.

And, oh God, do I want to hear what'll come out?

'Look, Conor,' he said, seizing on a useful

118

lie, just as he might have done across an interview-room table. 'I know you were there. You were seen. Harrison Academy uniform's unmistakable. A man with asthma, sitting at his open window in Percival Road, saw you round there.'

There. The direct accusation. Or not far from it.

What now?

'But — Well, yes. If you do know . . . Yes, I was there.'

'And?'

He dared not ask more.

Conor shifted further round in his seat till he was almost facing him directly as he drove.

'Dad,' he said, 'I'm sorry, but I can't tell you why I was there. I just can't.'

And he left it at that.

Impasse.

Had he had him in that interview room, tape machine running, statutory Appropriate Adult present as with any Juvenile, as the law called youngsters under seventeen, then he would have unhesitatingly gone on to press for an answer.

And would have got one, with all the consequences that would follow.

But here he was, Conor's father talking to Conor as he drove him to school. All right, their talk had got on to sticky territory. But so did many conversations between fathers and teenage children. Sudden obstinate silences more or less par for the course.

So let that be the situation now.

Anyhow, I need time to think. To think what I'm going to do. Offer up my son — my son — to police questioning, a charge of murder? Or . . . ? Or could I possibly bring myself to be an accessory? See what I can do to get him off the hook? Out of the country even? Anything.

I must think. I must.

So in silence, a sulky silence that almost could be felt, they sat until he drew up outside the familiar tall black-painted gates of Harrison Academy.

He did not say goodbye. Without looking back, Conor tramped through the gates with other arriving pupils. He thought he saw Belinda Withrington, with a boy he recalled as one of Conor's particular friends, tall, gangling Alec Gaffney, his bright red hair bobbing high over the others' heads. But Conor seemed to be deliberately avoiding them.

Iron-bound under down-weighing guilt?

But back to the Incident Room. Whatever was happening between himself and Conor, the investigation of Professor Unwala's murder was still continuing. And it was his duty to be taking part in it.

But how can I do more than appear to be taking part?

Yet the pace of the inquiry, it was obvious, had slowed almost to a standstill. The Gill had gone off, 'scattering orders like confetti at a wedding' as Jumbo put it, to re-interview wheezy Mr Jones. Presumably he hoped to persuade him to state the fog-dimmed black-coated figure he had seen was actually wearing a Britforce long mackintosh. Doorstepping the 'bad lads' had produced nothing more. The house-to-house round the murder scene had finally been abandoned, its ever-widening circles exhausted. The report on the cricket bat had come in, and, as was expected, no fingerprints had been retrieved from its perished and sodden rubber handle, any more than usable prints had been found on the bolts of the french windows at the scene. Only the blood on the bat had been confirmed as being the same group as Professor Unwala's. And whose else would it have been?

So he sat there at his table, pretending to be going through once again the reports of the day before and wondering what on earth he was to do. Conor a killer. It was impossible to believe. But what to make of his attitude in the car just now?

If the boy hadn't been at Professor Unwala's, what on earth had he been doing down in Sandymount? He had been there. He had admitted unequivocally that he had, before clamming up in that fashion. So surely, absurdly mysterious as that, he must have something to hide. And, with a murder committed in the very place he said he had been in, what was more obvious than that he had —

He stopped.

What was yet more obvious than that Conor had committed the murder? Well, perhaps it was as obvious that someone known to Conor was the killer. Or even that Conor feared someone he had met in Sandymount was that killer. Someone who perhaps had learnt from him that Professor Unwala might know where the Hampton Hoard was buried.

But who would that be? Who might Conor have encountered in Sandymount last summer? In those happy days, just before the break-up with Vicky, when he had come back from the dunes evening after evening, exhausted, hungry and ever more sunburnt, to wolf down as much supper as Vicky could cook. And had talked and talked. But not, surely, about anyone he had met. Or not by name. It had all really been about his finds, the coins from thirty or forty years ago and one or two from further back, a Victorian ring, and, once, a medallion with the motto *Drunkenness Expels Reason*. They had laughed over that, all three of them, and over the less exotic objects his machine had signalled, bottle tops and silver foil. Last summer when there were the three of them together.

And by then was Vicky already going with sports-mad Mike?

Yes, Conor could well have become friendly with fellow enthusiasts down there, however little he had mentioned any actual names. And if it was one of these friends he had talked to after leaving school on Monday, might he not feel obliged to say nothing about them? It was to his credit, in a way. Loyalty.

The thing now was to establish whether he had parted company from this friend, whoever he was, and been safely back home — *home,* that word for Mike and Vicky's cottage again — well before Mrs Ahmed heard that shout *You black bastard.*

How to find out? Easy. Ask my wife. My soon-to-be-ex-wife. Conor's mother.

A sudden shadow loomed over him.

'Well, Mr Benholme, have you come to any conclusions from your deep study of that report?'

It was the Gill, back from his visit to Mr Jones, standing just behind him looking down sharp-eyed at the report he had not actually been reading. He looked at it himself now.

Oh God, that old original report on Mr Jones. Embarrassment could get no worse.

'Well, no, sir — that is, yes. Yes, a possible lead has occurred to me.'

An inspiration. A get-out.

No need at this moment to tell the Gill what he had come to believe about Conor. Almost to believe. When he was more sure of the facts it would be another matter. If, say, he had found Conor had not got back to the cottage till well after six on Monday . . . But that did not bear thinking about.

For now he could simply repeat to the Gill the first thought that had come to him at yesterday's final briefing when March had made her point about 'the black coat'. If he was to say the lurker in the fog might have been a boy from Harrison Academy, the Gill could either laugh the notion to scorn or take him up on it. If the Gill shot down the whole idea, perhaps that would justify protecting Conor, especially if he was only protecting a friend. On the other hand, if the Gill agreed with the idea, he could suggest he should make inquiries himself. Former Harrison boy, knowing the set-up there.

And then, instead, I'll go to see Vicky. To find out, yes or no, whether Conor did get back to the cottage by six o'clock on Monday.

Chapter Eight

The Gill, lips pursed thoughtfully under little foxy moustache, pronounced the Harrison pupil line just worth following up. Out
at the cottage he found Vicky, wearing an
apron new to him, a stupid red plastic affair
with SLAVE WOMAN printed on it in big
black letters. At once she said sharply she
was busy. If he had anything to say he could
come into the kitchen.

Except for that apron, he thought with a
jet of emotion half anger, half regret, she
looks just the way she used to, preparing
meals in our own kitchen. Still very pretty
at — what is it? — thirty-eight. Hair in the
ponytail she's had it in for years. Pale narrow face coming down to that pointed chin,
ever-alert blue eyes under their blonde eyebrows, wide mouth as always a slash of
scarlet lipstick.

He felt a momentary flicker of desire.
Which she instantly extinguished.

'I might as well tell you straight away,'

she said, taking up a knife and forcefully slicing a strip of white fat off the meat on the chopping board in front of her, 'if you've come here to moan about divorce you've come to the wrong place.'

'No. No, it's not that at all.'

He paused, uncertain how to embark on telling her. Whether he could tell her at all.

'Well, what is it then, for heaven's sake? Can't you ever make up your mind about anything?'

I wish to God I could've already made up my mind about Conor. Can he really have tried to make Professor Unwala say where his wife had located the Hampton Hoard? Done that appalling thing? Or is he just loyally protecting someone he thinks may have killed the old man?

And bloody Vicky, why does she always want everything served up to her instantly?

But she does. Always has. Part of her attraction. Or was when we first met. Decisive Vicky. Her certainties. Something fixed among the ever-changing ways of seeing why people do what they do. And I owe something to that certainty of hers. Without her unquestioning push I doubt if I'd ever have made DCI.

'Well?'

'Yes. Well, it's this. It's about Conor.'

127

'Conor? Are you attempting to claim some rights in him? I thought we'd agreed it was better for him to be with me.'

Agreed? Hardly. You said it, and I thought you were probably right and I let him go. And, damn it, once again you're jumping in, mind made up, and getting it all wrong.

'No. No, it's not a question of where Conor's living.'

It's a question of: has he committed a murder?

But how can I say that?

'For Christ's sake, Phil, can't you come out with it, whatever it is? God, how your dithering used to get on my nerves.'

Not once upon a time it didn't. I can remember. *Phil, Phil, what I love about you is the way you always, always think before you go judging anybody.* And that wasn't dithering.

But, all right, if you want it crudely here it is.

'Listen, I'm worried to death about Conor. You know we've had a murder? Down in Sandymount?'

'For God's sake, why do you always think I know nothing? I do listen to the news, you know. I'm not a complete moron. It was some scientist from the year dot. Nobel

Prize or something. Right?'

Jumping in again. But better clear this out of the way.

'Yes. Yes, that's it, Professor Edul Unwala.'

'Well, what the hell has that got to do with Conor? Jesus, Phil, what's got into you today? You're worse than ever.'

He felt a flare of temper. Quelled it.

'Look, Vicky,' he said, forcing himself to sound reasonable. 'This is serious. It may be a very serious matter indeed. Do you know where Conor was on Monday evening?'

She shot him a look mingling anger and suspicion.

'What's all this about? You know where Conor would have been on Monday. This is term time, isn't it? We've agreed that this is the year he's got to begin getting down to serious work. He won't get to university if you go on indulging him. Him and his stupid treasure hunting.'

With an effort he ignored that.

'You're saying Conor was here?' he asked. 'Here doing his homework?'

A tiny shoot of hope sprang up.

'Why shouldn't he have been here?'

Wait. No.

No, this is a typical Vicky ploy when she's

in the wrong. The answer that can be taken two ways. And which almost always means it should be taken the worse way. She just can't help doing it. Same all our married life. God, even before we were married, though I was too much in love then to see it for what it was. But there it is, Vicky's way.

But this time I've got to straighten her out. I owe it to Conor.

'Listen, I've got to know the truth about this. It's important. Was Conor here all the time from when he got back from Harrison till when he went to bed? Yes or no?'

'What the hell is this? Listen, Phil Benholme, you may be a bloody detective, but that doesn't give you the right to go treating your wife as if she's a suspect down at that nick of yours.'

Back to that. To me being a detective. To the hard time I'm supposed to have given her because of that. Supposed? No, I did give her a hard time. Of course I did. I had to. And I know how she must have felt.

But — But that was then. This is now. Conor. And I've got to know. Not for my sake. For his.

He shook lingering doubts away.

'Vicky, I'm sorry. But I have got to have

130

a straightforward answer. Did Conor come directly back here after school on Monday?'

'Sorry. You're sorry. Once again. If you only bloody knew how that attitude infuriates me. Christ, do you know, I saw you last week walking through the Town Hall gardens, and you stepped off the path because there were some pigeons pecking at breadcrumbs there. Pigeons. You stepped aside for some bloody pigeons.'

Did I? I probably did. Well, why not? They were happily eating. No skin off my nose to step aside.

'Never mind about me and pigeons. This is Conor I'm talking about. Your son. Listen, for God's sake. What you say may affect the whole of his life.'

And now he had got through to her.

He saw the sudden look of dismay, or something worse, on her face. And at last she produced a proper answer to his question.

'Well, yes, I suppose Conor wasn't back by half past four that day. Monday. No, he wasn't. Definitely. I remember.'

'So when did he get back? Exactly? Try to be sure.'

She actually stopped and thought.

Not like my Vicky. My Vicky of old. No longer my Vicky.

'Phil, I can't say when it was exactly. Why have you got to know? What is this?'

His turn now to think. To think what words to use to tell Conor's mother her son was possibly a murderer.

'Look, love, a terrible thing. At least I think it is. I think it may be.'

'What is it? Phil, what?'

The anxiety shrill in her voice.

'Listen, I was saying, about the murder. In Sandymount.'

'For God's sake —'

She came to a flat halt.

'Phil, you're not saying Conor had anything to do with that? You can't be. You're trying to tell me that Conor, *Conor,* was involved in some sordid — Are you telling me Conor killed that old man, the Nobel whatsit?'

'Yes. Or, well, no. Oh God, I don't know. But there's evidence. Good evidence. Evidence that with anyone else would have me, as a detective, wanting to pull them in for questioning. At the very least.'

'My God, Phil, what's got into you? It's police work, that's what it is. It's being a damn detective. Suspicion. Suspecting everybody. You're going mad, do you know that?'

No, I don't. I'm not going mad, or anything like it. This is just Vicky kicking against the pricks, in any way she knows how. Christ, I can understand how she feels, hearing what I've just told her. What did I feel like myself when the thought first came into my head? But it's not just some wild fantasy. There's too much about it that's solid fact. Conor's evasiveness. His anxiety to know the details when I first mentioned the murder to him. His admitting he lied. His refusal to tell me anything more. There's even the size of his bloody shoes.

He took a deep breath.

The thing is not to get riled with Vicky. To remember to try and understand what her feelings must be. But, somehow, to get out of her the accurate facts about Conor on Monday evening.

'Listen, darling —'

'I am not your bloody darling, Phil Benholme. If I ever was, you've lost all right to call me that. You drove me out. Understanding me. Always claiming to know what I was thinking. Tolerating me. Well, you've fucking understood me to death. So shut up. Shut up, and bloody go.'

'No. You know I can't go. Not till you've told me, calmly and as accurately as you can, what time it was that Conor got back here on Monday.'

And again it seemed he had suddenly pierced the cloud of fear and hatred between them.

'What time he got back?' she answered, all the edgy hysteria gone from her voice. 'Let me see. It must have been about six . . .'

His heart leapt up. Six. Mrs Ahmed certain she had heard the *You black bastard* yell at almost exactly six. So if Conor was here, three miles, no, four from Percival Road, then it couldn't have been him who brought that ancient cricket bat savagely down.

'About six? How near either side? How do you know exactly what time it was?'

'Christ, Phil, stop bullying. You're not in one of your interview rooms now. Just let me think.'

Strange reversal. Vicky wanting time to think. Impulsive Vicky. But let her have every bit as long as she wants. If she comes up with some good reason for knowing Conor was here at six on Monday or soon enough after, then the whole world will look different. For both of us.

'Take your time, take your time.'

'Yes. Yes, I know now. It depends on when Mike came back home from work. He generally gets in about six. And did he on Monday . . . ? Let me think.'

He suppressed the feelings the word *home* in connection with Vicky and Mike had once more sent flaring up.

If bloody Mike coming home at six proves beyond doubt that Conor was here shortly after, then I'll forgive him everything. Forgive both of them everything. After all, Vicky did have cause to feel that I wasn't the husband she was entitled to.

'Yes. Yes, Mike was here. And I remember he said something about his boss, that stupid Mr Phillips, wanting him to stay on and how he'd said "Up yours" to him. So, yes, he was here just before six.'

'And Conor? When did he come in? Before Mike or after?'

She thought again.

'Well, he definitely came in after Mike. I remember Mike said something to him about being late, and his homework, and Conor lost his temper and shouted at him that it was none of his business whether he did his homework or not.'

For a moment he was deflected. Conor resenting his substitute father? Hankering for his real one?

But then another thought, an uglier one. Conor losing his temper. Had that been the second time within perhaps an hour that he had lost his temper? Had he lost it more completely, utterly, down in that house in Percival Road? Had the blanking-out rage that had made him bring that bat down on Professor Unwala, half-evaporated, spewed up again when Mike had rebuked him?

The time? It all depends on the exact time Conor had got here, to this house. How long would it take him to come from Percival Road to Frogs Lane? No direct bus, and he'd have had no transport of his own. So he would have had to have walked. Or run? If he'd just killed Professor Unwala, had tried to conceal the crime by moving that bookcase, had then rushed out into the garden, had vomited in horror at what he had done — yes, that fitted Conor — and if he had then climbed over that fence leaving the footmark and had stuffed the bat under the bush by the throughway, how long would all that take before he could get to the house here? Four miles away, probably nearer four and a half if he had had to start in Seabray Way. So how long? Running, say? Twenty-five minutes? He couldn't have done it in much less.

'OK,' he said cautiously. 'Mike, you say, got in about six. Was it a little before or a little after? And how much later than him was Conor?'

'You're crowding me again, Phil.'

'I'm sorry, I'm sorry. But this is important. Vital.'

He left her to think.

At least she didn't round on me for once again saying *sorry*. Give her credit for that. But can't she make up her mind? Ten minutes after Mike? Twenty even, if Mike got here a bit before six? Everything would be all right then. But just when had Mike got here?

A sudden thought. When she said she knew about the murder she'd claimed she kept up with the news. Watched it on TV. So had she been watching ITV at twenty to six on Monday, like Mrs Ahmed in her Pakistani-packed house? And had Mike watched with her?

'Listen, do you watch the news in the early evening? ITV or BBC? And were you watching on Monday?'

Again she thought, biting at her scarlet lower lip.

'I don't know,' she said at last with a touch of petulance. 'Sometimes I switch on, sometimes I don't. Mike doesn't much care for it, unless there's some sports result he's interested in.'

'But Monday? Can't you remember?' He was almost shouting, but couldn't stop himself.

'No. No, I bloody well can't remember. If Mike was back a little before six I'd have switched off if I'd had ITV on. Or I wouldn't have switched on for the six o'clock BBC news. You can't have everything your own way, you know.'

'Damn it, it's not my way I want. It's Conor. It's important to know if he was here at the time of the murder down in Sandymount. We know exactly when that was.'

'Well, listen to me, Phil Benholme. I can't believe it really can be important to know about Conor. He's not a murderer. So it can't matter. However much so-called evidence you've got. Evidence against your own son, Christ.'

He strove for patience.

She is his mother after all. She's bound to feel the way she does. Facts or no facts.

'Come on, love. Just put yourself back to Monday. Where were you when Mike came in? Start from there.'

Suddenly a purely vicious gleam came into her eyes.

'I'll tell you where I was. Or where I was just two minutes after Mike came in. I was in the bedroom. On the bloody bed. And Mike was on top of me. There.'

Is she saying that just to hit at me? Out of a sort of guilt? She could be. It'd be just like her. Just like her the way she was when the marriage began really breaking up.

Outside, a municipal dustcart was backing into a driveway before turning round. *Attention. Attention. This vehicle is reversing.* That honking mechanical loudspeaker voice.

But it had distracted him just enough to be able to decide to take her outburst as being the simple truth.

'All right, if you were, you were. But that must mean that Conor got back here a good bit after six, for Mike to have had a go at him like that.'

He pulled himself back from adding *Or did he do it while he was lying on top of you trousers round under his bum?*

'Oh, very well. We weren't doing it, if you must know. Not that we don't. As often as possible.'

'Right then, I imagine you were both next door in the sitting room. And you hadn't watched the news. But Mike had just come in, saying he was back as usual at more or less six having said Up yours to his Mr Phillips, or possibly not. So how long had Mike been back when Conor came in and got blasted about his homework?'

139

'I don't know. It was a bit after Mike had got home.'

'How much of a bit?'

A shrug.

'I suppose a quarter of an hour, twenty minutes. We don't sit there looking at the clock all the time, you know. Whatever else we might or might not be doing.'

He did some arithmetic. Conor back here then at six-fifteen, or six-twenty. Right, if he had been in that room at number twelve Percival Road at just before six when Mrs Ahmed heard the scream, he could not have got here, even running all the way, in less than half an hour. Certainly not if he'd stopped to puke in the garden there.

So he was OK, off the hook.

He felt relief welling up inside him. Slowly, as if he could not dare let it flood out.

'Or it might have been longer. We were having a drink. I think I was on to my second.'

Oh, God.

'How much longer, for God's sake?'

He could not now keep the anger out of his voice.

And she replied with an equal anger.

'I don't know. I don't bloody well know, I keep telling you. It might have been twenty

140

minutes. It might have been half an hour. It might have been even more. But one thing I do know: Conor did not kill that Nobel person. He did not. He did not.'

But, he thought, blackness coming back in, denser, darker than before, he may have done. My son. He may have done, if that's all the alibi he's got.

Chapter Nine

He drove away from the cottage at full speed. When he had finally made clear to Vicky that, without the alibi she was unable to give Conor, he had to believe their son could well have killed Professor Unwala, she had spat and splattered at him till he could take it no longer. But as soon as he had rounded the corner out of Frogs Lane he brought the car to a halt.

One thing, he thought, if I drive in the state I'm in now I'll be more of a danger than if I'd got nine or ten pints sloshing in my gut.

'My God, I knew when I married you, Phil Benholme, you were a cold fucking fish. But I never in a million years imagined you'd shop your own son on a charge of murder.'

That had been one of Vicky's milder taunts.

But did I deserve them? Do I deserve them? Is what I know I really ought to do such a totally unthinkable thing? For God's sake, I told the stupid bitch: if it was anyone else that I'd found with as much evidence against them I'd have unhesitatingly pulled them in. So why should it be different with Conor?

It is, though. My son. I'm faced with going to the Gill and telling him I believe my son could well be our murderer. Worse, the murderer of a Nobel Prize winner, a killer the media will be crying out to have 'brought to justice'. And, Christ, yes, there's the press conference at eleven.

He looked at his watch.

Twenty-to.

So what I really ought to do this minute is drive back as quickly as I can, find the Gill and report to him that we could be bringing in a suspect — *It is understood that a youth is helping the police with their inquiries* — even as he is fielding reporters' questions. He'd be fucking delighted. Another triumph in the making for Detective Chief Superintendent Fothergill, soon to be Assistant Chief Constable, and before long Deputy Chief Constable and bloody Chief Constable.

And Conor?

Picturing Conor, once the Gill had learnt the strength of the evidence against him, was, for all that he knew every detail of the safeguards the boy would have, something he could not bring himself to do.

With face set rigid he put the car into gear, took off.

But he arrived only just in time for the conference. Lucky from two points of view. First, there was no opportunity to put his suspicions, his unbelievable suspicions, to the Gill, and second, he just avoided the wrath that would have jetted out had he not been ready to go marching on to the platform behind the Gill to take his place next to the force public relations officer. Red-hot on punctuality, Detective Chief Superintendent Fothergill. Especially when the TV cameras were there.

But insistence on punctuality, to do the Gill justice, no bad thing in a senior police officer.

The conference began much as he had expected. A good many more reporters present than at most such affairs. Three TV camera crews. Half a dozen photographers crouching on one knee at the front punctuating the proceedings with camera flashes. And plenty of questions after the Gill's punchily delivered opening statement. The Gill pretty good at taking them, too. Sharp, in control. The very image of a decidedly up-to-date top police officer.

And then came a question from the muck-raking *New Star*.

'Is the investigation taking into account the fact that Professor Unwala, despite his long retirement, was still engaged in major research, and was very near making a break-through on Alzheimer's disease?'

It brought him bolt upright. At once he tried to make it look as if, uncomfortable on his slatted wooden folding chair, he had just been shifting his weight. Those sharp-eyed buggers from the nationals would be quick to take an uneasy movement as an indication that no one in this provincial force had cottoned on. And how had the *New Star* got to hear about Professor Un-wala's research, typically grafting on an im-minent 'breakthrough' of which there was in reality no sign?

Oh, yes. Got it. My fault, in a way. Men-tioning that the professor had been working on Alzheimer's at the briefing last night, trying to infuse an extra sympathetic ur-gency. Some bright spark must have thought of making a few quid passing on a tip. Which of them read the *New Star*? Almost all of them, favourite paper in the lower ranks. And upwards. Not the most enlight-ened group in the community, the men and women of Barshire police.

But then their work was hardly conducted in enlightening circumstances. Their work: our work: my work.

Then, after the Gill had snapped that, naturally, this was something the inquiry was taking into consideration, there had come a wicked little supplementary 'And are you aware, Chief Superintendent, that there is in King's Hampton at the present time a team from a well-known German pharmaceutical company?'

The *New Star*, in its customary little-Britain way, going for some fantastic wicked Germans angle. And, as was perhaps to be expected, the Gill passed that one on.

'I suggest that is something the officer in charge of King's Hampton CID is best positioned to answer. Detective Chief Inspector Benholme?'

Miraculously, as he got to his feet, rather slowly, he remembered something he had read in the *Advertiser*.

'Yes, King's Hampton police are, of course, aware of the presence in the town of distinguished guests from Germany. They are here for talks with one of the major firms on our industrial estate, Hampton Pharmaceuticals.'

And, if I'm not mistaken, a definite look

of disappointment on that pale-faced reporter. I may be soft as a duck's arse, but I do know what's going on around me.

With Barshire Police shown to be fully on top of local conditions, if not much advanced with finding who had killed Professor Unwala, the conference broke up.

So now, he thought to himself, it's time for me, far from soft, to go to Fothergill and inform him that the Harrison Academy boy asthmatic Mr Jones saw in the fog was very likely my son Conor ready to commit murder.

To put off the evil moment rather than because of any physical need, he decided to visit the toilets.

There, standing four-square at one of the urinals was Jumbo Hastings, and a sudden idea came to him. He had wondered if there was anyone he could discuss his dilemma with. A fellow officer was the only possibility. No one outside the police could assess the evidence in the same way. And, up till now, he had rejected everybody. Bob Carter? Too ready with the instant judgment. Anyone lower in rank, an unfair burden to put on them. Waiting for Mr Verney back from Bramshill? Too much the set-in-his-ways old-fashioned detective. Go by the book, would be his advice. And going by the book would be taking what he knew directly to the officer at the head of the inquiry. Detective Chief Superintendent Fothergill. Which was precisely what he wanted to find reasons not to have to do.

But Jumbo? All right, junior in rank, and destined to stay that way. Happy to. But not junior in experience. A detective before he had been one himself.

Yes, Jumbo.

The flush went in one of the cubicles, and a moment later its door was opened and the Gill himself came out.

Stepping quickly up to the urinal next to Jumbo, he stood head lowered pretending not even to notice the big boss. Not the moment to receive a word of congratulation on the way he had handled the *New Star* reporter. If one would be forthcoming.

Then as soon as the outer door had wheezed closed he turned to Jumbo.

'Something I wanted to talk to you about. In private.'

Jumbo wriggled away his penis, zipped himself up, stepped away.

'So long as no one comes barging in, this is what they call a fine and private place.'

Jumbo, poetry quoter. Surprise, surprise. Well, no. Probably just some scrap he's picked up somewhere. But, in any case, if it's a sign of a well-stored mind that's just what's required.

'You're right at that,' he said.

Then he took the plunge.

'Look, Jumbo, something terrible's happened to me.'

Jumbo gave him a sharp glance, thrusting his big, florid face forward. Perhaps a joke contemplated. But, plain to see, the idea being rejected.

'Tell Uncle then. What you want, isn't it?'

'Yes. Yes, by God, it is. Someone to tell.'

'So?'

So it came out. The moment when DS March had shot out her query about the black-coat lurker in the fog and he had suddenly thought of Harrison Academy boys in their black jackets, worn out of bravado in all weathers, and what that said about how evasive Conor had been when he had first told him about the murder.

'You see . . . Well, you see, I think it may be Conor himself we're looking for.'

Jumbo's large, placid face creased in a frown.

'Listen, Phil, are you sure you're not making too much of something not really all that evident?'

'I wish I were, Jumbo. I wish I were. But

149

there's more. A lot more. I mean, for one thing . . . Well, you know Vicky and I have split up?'

'Yes, of course. But what you yourself probably don't realize is quite how hard that's hit you. Oh, you've not shown many signs of it, that's not your way. But anyone who's known you as long as I have could see it. You're hyped up, Phil. Oversensitive. You don't mind me saying that?'

But it came as shock. A slap in the face.

He stood there, suddenly aware of the sharp medicinal tang of the toilets' disinfectant.

Yes. Well, good old Jumbo. A true friend, someone who'd been quietly caring.

But is it true, what he said? Well, yes. Yes, I suppose it is. The break-up has hit me. Even harder than I'd admitted.

'No, Jumbo, of course I don't mind. Thanks for saying it.'

He brought his thoughts back to what he had been trying to put into words.

'But listen. Honestly there's more to what I've come to think about Conor than just some overwrought ideas of my own. I mean, there's Conor's overwrought ideas for one thing. Or the overwrought ideas he may have been keeping suppressed. Down there. A split-up like ours doesn't leave an only child untouched, you know. Especially one of Conor's age.'

'Granted. But still, if that's all . . .'

'No, it isn't all. There's evidence, hard evidence, to back up my suspicions, I promise you. Think. What about that yell Mrs Ahmed heard? She said a boy's voice, "I am knowing what is sounding like a boy". I can hear her now.'

'Well, all right. She heard a boy's voice, and you've said she's a good witness. But that doesn't mean it was Conor's voice. For God's sake, Phil, there are other boys in King's Hampton. Thousands of 'em. Girls, too, come to that. And, after Di March got back from Barminster full of how she'd been looking at some Britforce trooper's black and blue arse, the field's wide open. You know it is.'

'All right, it may be down to some youngster in the town again. But how many of those wear size seven trainers? Conor does.'

'OK, he does. And that cuts the number of possibles from, say, five thousand to three thousand.'

'Nevertheless . . . Look. I'm really not being paranoid about this. The trainers and the yell Mrs Ahmed heard are only a couple of strands in the evidence.'

'OK, if you say so. But go on. You'd best

get the whole of it off your chest while you're about it.'

Jumbo looked across at the heavy door of the toilets. No sign of anyone pushing at it.

'Right. Well, don't think I didn't ask myself why my Conor should have killed Professor Unwala. No connection. That was my first reaction. Till I remembered.'

'Well, what? What did you remember?' Jumbo allowed the full weight of his scepticism to roll with the words.

'Just this. The Hampton Hoard. You must know about —'

'Don't I just. Famous million-quid's worth of gold coins buried in the dunes. Roman, Celtic, I don't know. Whatever. But that's no more than the sort of silly rumour people love to persuade themselves is true.'

'Exactly. To persuade themselves. And what's more likely than Conor — he's always been mad about treasure hunting — has persuaded himself in the same way? And he could easily have got to learn, true or false, that Mrs Unwala, who had a degree in archaeology, had located the Hoard but died before she could get to it. And then he could very well have been tempted by the idea of becoming an instant archaeological success.'

'Stop. Now listen, Phil, you're building

castles in the air. Castles? More like bloody dungeons. Come off it. Think who you're talking about. Conor. Your son. I do know him, you know. I've seen him off and on since he was at primary school. A decent lad, if ever there was.'

'No, Jumbo. Listen, I've talked to him about it all. I went out specially first thing in the morning and gave him a lift into school, just so that I could clear it up. If I could.'

'Well? Why didn't you?'

'Because the damn boy first of all denied being in Sandymount on Monday evening, though he said he'd been down there when I first happened to mention the murder. And then when I tricked him, best bloody interrogator-fashion, into admitting he'd told me a lie, he just one hundred per cent clammed up. Clammed up tight. Now, if that doesn't show he ought to be questioned, and by someone like the Gill, then what does?'

Jumbo thrust his lower lip forward doubtfully.

'Yeah. Yeah, that's the worst thing you've found to say so far. But — But even then, Phil, it's not proof. Nothing like proof. I tell you what, the boy may have been down in Sandymount at the time all right, but he

153

could be covering up for a mate. Can't think why, but he may be.'

'Oh, I've already thought of that. But even if it should turn out to be the explanation, I still ought to tell the Gill. I mean, if Conor's concealing evidence about a murder, he should be made to talk.'

'Well, even if you're right about that, Conor's not really involved. I dare say I could get him to tell me his mate's name, if you like.'

'No. No, it could still be the other way round, him the killer. Don't you see that?'

'No, Phil, frankly I don't. Of course I don't know Conor as well as you do, but I just don't see him as a murderer. I just don't. Not even as the result of a sudden burst of rage. If it had been that, he'd have confessed to it. Like a shot.'

'Oh, I don't know. I'd like to believe you. Of course I bloody would. But if it's true . . . I hoped earlier on he might have an alibi. The time he got back to Vicky's new place. But he hasn't. I went into it all with her. Had a hell of an upper-and-downer in the end. Naturally. But it's quite clear: Conor was in Sandymount at around six on Monday and he lied to me about it for as long as he could and then just clammed up. No, it's no good. He's a suspect. He must be. The prime suspect in fact. There's no one else.'

'But, Phil, think. It's early days yet. How many other cases we've worked on produced no real suspect until weeks had gone by? No, Phil, listen to me. There's no need whatsoever to go to the Gill. No need at all.'

Which was when he decided, without uttering another word, that he would do just that.

Chapter Ten

'Well, Mr Benholme, you realize what this means?'

The Gill, sitting stiffly upright behind Benholme's own desk, glowered into the mid-distance.

'I'll have to come off the case, sir. Yes.'

'More than that, Mr Benholme. You ought to be suspended. Suspended until the outcome of this is clear, and then most probably be asked to consider your future in the force.'

No.

No, no, no, no. For better or worse, this is my life. The life I've even sacrificed my marriage to. The life that may even have been the root cause of my son becoming a murderer. But it's what I've always wanted to do. Ever since that day, when I was still at Harrison, when I decided, never thinking of it before, to go into the police.

For a single moment, stretching in his head to many more, he recalled the circumstances. Peter Watson's nan. His stories about her cantankerous ways. They had entertained the whole class. Particularly that tale of the dyed-in-the-wool card player's affronted reaction when, coming back from her whist drive, she had found she had been burgled. It had sent them all into stitches. He himself had wondered for a while if Peter, who had often suffered at her tongue's end, had been the home-wrecking intruder, so graphic was his description. All the emptied drawers, the spattered contents of jars and pots, the dozens of long-kept hats pulled out of their boxes and stuck up here and there over the whole house. But a few days later Peter had said the old lady had been taken to hospital after a heart attack, and suddenly the intrusion into her privacy had become vivid in his mind. A flash of revelation. *I won't go into the tax office like Dad. I'll go into the police.*

And now it's all in jeopardy. The Gill plainly thinks there's a good case against Conor and that the father of a killer hasn't got any sort of a police career. The bastard. Never a hint that there may be two sides to this, that what I told him — and, Jesus, I shouldn't have done, Jumbo was right — is really purely circumstantial. But, no, already in his mind he's got Conor questioned, charged, brought to court, found guilty. All with scarcely drawing a breath.

'However, I suppose the points you've drawn to my attention are to some extent circumstantial. Not that what old Henry Thoreau said years ago hasn't got a great deal of truth in it. "Some circumstantial evidence is very strong, as when you find a trout in the milk". And I'm very much afraid, Mr Benholme, that your son's been trying to sell you milk mixed with more than a little river water.'

'I think there is a case to be made going the other way, sir. I mean you —'

'Yes, well, no doubt anything that tends towards the boy not being guilty, if there is anything, will come out when he's properly questioned. However, I think, taking everything into account, perhaps we'll delay a decision about suspending you. I'm not sure I could justify it to our financial masters, for one thing. The work has to get done. But, understand, although you will be here on duty, you are not to speak to any other officer about any aspect of this investigation whatsoever. You are off the case.'

Well, bastard or no bastard, I can't deny he's seen there may be two sides to it. Even if with the greatest reluctance.

The Gill gave a sharp cough.

'And for that reason,' he added, 'it's perhaps a good thing that I've asked the Chief to have Mr Verney recalled from his course at Bramshill. He'll be taking over the investigation from myself. I've got more than enough on my plate at Headquarters, as you can imagine.'

'Yes, sir.'

The thing to say. And me not in a position to do anything but keep my head down and *Yes, sir* and *No, sir* him till this cloud is lifted. As, please God, it will be. As it must be. But, the crafty sod, back to HQ when it looks as if there isn't going to be any instant triumph for whizz-kid Detective Chief Superintendent Fothergill. His Britforce angle looking plain silly as soon as Di March started telling her tale about that thuggish trooper's backside.

Sitting at his desk in his reclaimed office — it had given him only a momentary satisfaction, to jerk into the waste bin the Gill's pipe ashes — he was finding it now only too easy to imagine the scene taking place in the Custody Suite. The Custody officer, pompous, fussy, I-go-by-the-book Sergeant Spage, meticulously sorting out a Custody record sheet. The way he goes like a busy squirrel through a sheaf of identical blank forms to find the sole one he thinks right. And now, with each section of the selected sheet solemnly filled in — no one writes more carefully — he'll first consult his watch, then the clock and finally his watch once more before inscribing the time on the sheet and, with even more care, signing it.

What will Conor make of all that ritual, standing in front of Spage's table? Will he jab out some smart teenage crack? Probably not. Poor Conor, bound to be intimidated by the scrubbed-clean, bleak inhumanity of the Custody Suite, the faint ever-present odour of antiseptic seeping out from the cells beyond. Let alone, looming behind him, by the massive form of the arresting officer, Detective Superintendent Verney, broad-shouldered battle tank, heavy of jaw, jutting eyebrows touched with grey, a bit of a middle-age belly but one more like a battering ram than a place to stow fish and chips.

Soon Conor should, according to the laid-down procedure, be informed of his statutory rights. Or had he already been told them? Spage sing-songing out the prescribed words in that mechanical way. A solicitor? Will Conor, bemused as he must be, have asked for one when told he could? Would Spage, ploughing away at getting it right beyond any possible criticism, have arranged for a solicitor? And under the provisions of the Children and Young Persons Act, he must have already informed 'a responsible person' that Conor, 'a juvenile', had been arrested. A responsible person? And who's the Number One person responsible for Conor? Me. Here. Sitting in my chair. Conor's father. Strictly warned by Detective Chief Superintendent Fothergill to avoid speaking to any other officer about any aspect of the case.

So, failing me, who? Conor's mother, of course. She wouldn't — she would never dare send bloody sports-mad Mike in her place?

He almost jumped up and rushed down to the Custody Suite, despite all that the Gill had said about not speaking to anyone.

Instead, defying that order just a little, he picked up his phone, got on to the Incident Room. Things would be quiet there now. Quiet but atmospherically tense, as he remembered from other major inquiries when they believed they were on the brink of a result. In what he hoped was a lightly disguised voice, he asked for DS Hastings.

'Jumbo, it's me. Listen, tell me quickly one more thing. Just a yes or no. Who's coming in as Appropriate Adult? Is it Vicky?'

'Yes.'

And down went the phone. Jumbo, sensibly, keeping his nose clean.

So Conor would have been solemnly informed of the grounds for his detention. *On suspicion of being involved in the murder of one Edul Unwala on Monday, 10 November last.* Something like that.

But, when he heard those words, would they come to him like a knell? The final confirmation that his crime had come to light? But, no. No, they must not. He is innocent. The words would have frightened him. Of course they would. But they would do no more than frighten him. Surely an innocent suspect.

Yet wasn't sheer fright sometimes enough to make someone innocent believe themselves guilty? Would fear, when it came to Verney's questioning, make Conor believe he might have done what he had not? Youngsters had been brought to that state in the past. Probably more than once by Verney's own no-quarter-given methods. Would Conor be able to stand up to the hours of bombardment? With only Vicky there to support him?

So, Vicky now on her way, or soon to be so, the procedures in the Custody Suite over at last. Spage requesting Conor's signature stating he had been told the grounds for his detention. Spage making sure he signed in the correct place. Once, bringing in some collar himself, there had been a fearful spat when Spage had seen the confirmatory signature being applied not exactly to the correct line.

But Conor? Where will he be waiting? Not in a cell. Provisions of the Code of Practice for the Detention, Treatment and Questioning, they'll mean that at his age he'll be in some room down there with just a simple lock on the door.

And what will he be thinking as he sits there? *Jesus, will they get it all out of me?* And the flood of cold sweat? Heart suddenly thumping and thumping? Or, almost as bad — not as bad, not as bad — will it be *My father, my own bleeding father, getting me accused of murder? Murder? Me? How could he even think such a thing?*

Then, eventually Vicky arriving. Spitting fire, no doubt. Fire directed at me? It will be at some time or another. And I can't say I blame her. But for now poor old By-the-Book Spage will get it.

I'd almost like to be there, fly on the wall, to see. But I wouldn't. I'd rather never know anything at all about it. I'd rather it all

163

wasn't happening. But it is. My Conor about to be interviewed by tank-crushing Detective Superintendent Verney.

The times I've sat beside him in interview rooms. Back even in the days when he was just a DI and I was at the beginning of my time in CID, some breaking-and-entering case or other. Me cast in the role of soft man against his hard man. In the days when there was no recording machine sitting there between Verney and his suspect. The hand opposite suddenly grasped, the fingers twisted back, the snarled insults. And finally, white-faced, the cough. Another one for the Crown Court, with evidence even the sharpest lawyer couldn't upset.

And Verney not much more civilized now that his every word goes down on the twin-tape.

Conor facing that. And not over some routine breaking-and-entering affair. But a murder inquiry.

He sat there, lips compressed like a trap. In case he wept.

He found at last he could not stay staring at the window opposite, seeing nothing. There was work he ought to be doing. On his restored desk there had been a full in-tray. It was hardly touched so far. How could he sit reading, initialling, filling the out-tray when he would have absorbed nothing?

But I've got to do something. I can't sit, going over and over what might be happening to Conor. What might be, and what might not. Verney may have left him to think things over. Or he may be pressing him like a roadroller squeezing and squeezing forward. Conor may be drinking a cup of tea, the statutory offered 'refreshment'. Or he may already be slumped over the table, his racking sobs recorded in duplicate by the softly whirring machine beside him.

I just don't know, and I've no way of finding out. Off the case. *Understand, although you will be here on duty, you are not to speak to any other officer about any aspect of this investigation whatsoever. You are off the case.* The Gill's mouth shutting in a tight line above that little reddish brush of moustache.

But I must do something. And there's only one thing I can possibly bring myself to do. Something to clear Conor. Or . . .

Or, face it, at worst to confirm my dread.

But what? I'm off the case. Off the case. And yet . . . Well, is there nothing I can do, not as a police officer, but as Conor's father? Damn it, if I wasn't in the police

165

and they had come along and arrested my son, wouldn't I be doing everything I could to clear him? A father's right.

So what to do? Try and see it rationally. Assume Conor is innocent. As he is. As he is. So, then, ask: why did he tell that damning lie about not being in Sandymount on Monday around six o'clock? Answer, I've already told myself, and, come to that, told old Jumbo, who thought it a reasonable guess. Conor must be shielding someone.

But wait. Wait. I assumed if he was shielding someone it was a fellow treasure hunter he'd met on the dunes. But there are other activities Sandymount is well known for. Such as the selling of drugs. In particular, in fact, of Ecstasy, bought in small handfuls by stupid teenagers intending to have a high time at a weekend rave. Can it be that Conor, for all that I'm almost a hundred per cent sure he isn't a user himself — Damn it, I do know the signs — has a friend who is? And, yes, he'd certainly want to cover for him. Not be a sneak.

And, if he does have such a mate, isn't it most probably a boy from Harrison? Right then, go along to the school, go along now and see the head. What's his name? Yes, Teploe. Question him about drug use in the school. There's bound to be some. There

166

is in every secondary school in the country, in quite a few primaries come to that. No. A better plan. Talk — I've been meaning to for weeks — about security at the school. And move on from there . . .

He was clattering down the stairs with his coat on, phone call made — 'Yes, Mr Teploe is still here, as a matter of fact' — almost before he had properly realized what he was doing.

Mr Teploe, long, lugubrious face, rimless glasses, sad greeny-black academic gown drooping down the length of his long body. A dusty raven.

'Well, yes, security is a problem, Chief Inspector. A problem, I don't deny it. All right, if we could put a tall electrified fence round the whole school and the playing fields, then we could perhaps tell ourselves there wouldn't be much to worry about. But we can't. Physically impossible. Out of the question on cost grounds. And even then, the evil man will find a way of sliding in.'

A sudden fixed expression on the long face revealing a fiercely moral outlook. *The evil man.* Not altogether pleasant? Someone like that in charge of four hundred adolescent boys and girls? But then shouldn't a headmaster have a moral outlook?

167

Question to be looked at some other time. But at the present moment a way in.

'Yes, I see what you mean. And I imagine on occasion you find evil, or wickedness at least, creeping in with some of your pupils themselves. That's something else, in fact, that I'd like to take the opportunity of discussing with you. Drug use. How much of it do you think goes on in the school? I'm not criticizing, you understand. It's something no one can altogether prevent. But I would like to know what you think the state of affairs is on that front here at Harrison.'

Mr Teploe's long face took on an even gloomier look.

'Well, I can't deny, Chief Inspector, that there has been drug taking in the school. We even had — what is it you call them? — a pusher among the pupils.'

'Oh, yes, sir. Was he — or was it a she — prosecuted? I don't think I recall the case.'

A puff of disparagement.

'No. No, Chief Inspector, we didn't think the affair warranted anything like that. The governors and I. We felt expulsion would meet the case. The young man was, in any case, shortly due to leave King's Hampton. Father in the Army, an overseas posting.'

Should be giving him a bit of stick, this

168

headmaster. But better not. Not if I'm really here only to find out who Conor may be protecting.

'But that was some time ago, yes? I'd be rather more interested in having an up-to-date picture. Do you in fact have any suspicions that anyone is pushing, say, cannabis, among the pupils now? Or is there activity outside the gates at the end of school that gives you any cause for concern?'

'Well, outside school bounds, Mr Benholme, I can't really be held responsible.'

'Not even when something may be happening just outside the gates?'

Don't let this sanctimonious bugger off too lightly. Was it a mistake to get Conor in to the old place? Father's footsteps? Always a hassle finding the fees. But a lot going for the old alma mater too. Best facilities by far for miles around, pretty good teachers by all accounts and a tradition of academic success. So, as usual, much to be said on both sides.

But how much to be said about drugs? About Conor and his friends?

'Yes, yes, of course, we do our best to keep our eyes open. But, you know, we can hardly go spying on our pupils.'

'No, of course, I recognize that. But I must tell you I am somewhat concerned. As much as a parent as a policeman.'

'Ah, well, there I can at least assure you that your son — Colum, isn't it? — is not one of the boys I would think of as likely to be in what we must learn to call, I fear, the drugs scene. No, a good lad. Near the top of his class, I believe, and a fine figure on the sports field.'

'Well, I'm glad to hear that.'

However little reassuring that sort of blather is. Colum? I'd love to Colum him. Still, I suppose with four hundred pupils he can't be expected to have full details at his fingertips about any one of them.

'But I was asking about the drugs situation in general. I mean, with your knowledge of the boys in the school, and the girls too, come to that, I expect you could, in strictest confidence, give me a name or two. They'll go no further unless we find something definite.'

'Yes.'

Mr Teploe came to a halt.

Is he going to name a name or two? Or is he going to stand there like a long black sodding raven and say nothing?

'Yes. Well, I suppose it is my duty to assist the police in whatever way I can. And so, yes. Yes, I could give you some names.'

'And they are . . . ?'

'Well, there was a boy by the name of Melton. He actually left us at the end of last academic year, and I understand he has obtained some sort of a job in London. But I dare say my secretary could give you an address, if that would be of any help.'

Dodging still. The good name of Harrison Academy. Doesn't he realize Harrison Academy may be acquiring a bad name as well?

'Perhaps it would be a help, sir. I'll make a point of asking your secretary. But you spoke about *some names*. Can you give me more?'

Mr Teploe sighed. Heavily and long.

'Well, I suppose — But please understand, I have nothing in the way of proof.'

Come on, come on.

'Yes, of course, sir, I understand that, and I've already assured you there's no question of any prosecution arising simply from the names you've given me. The names you're just about to give me.'

Putting all his determination into face and body language, he waited.

'Very well, Mr Benholme. At the end of last year, that is in July last, I had occasion to take disciplinary action against two boys, together with one of the girls, when a member of my staff observed them attempting to sell a small number of those tablets called, I understand, Ecstasy.'

Another silence.

'And they were?'

'Macaulay Stornier and Peter Vinberry. And the girl was Belinda Withrington, although I suspect she was more of an innocent involved rather than a full participant.'

'I see, sir. And thank you.'

But Belinda Withrington. Conor's Belinda. Even if she had been no more than that innocent accomplice to those two passers-on of E tablets, she was still a link, a possible link, between Conor and Sandymount drug dealing.

Chapter Eleven

A lead. The slightest of leads, granted. But a lead. If Conor's protecting someone who was down in Sandymount with him trying to buy some E, then isn't it at least likely that he's protecting Belinda Withrington? His girl. Or, maybe, his girl until just recently.

With a jolt of sharp irony he recalled, outside the once-familiar Harrison Academy gates oblivious of the dull penetrating cold, how just before his marriage began coming to its acrimonious end both he and Vicky had almost cooed with pleasure over the pair. Their son, little Conor, suddenly becoming a big boy, getting himself a real girlfriend. Becoming, if only just, a man. At that time he had stifled in Conor's interest his doubts about the Withrington girl. But doubts he had had. She had seemed too sophisticated for her age, and, even in the little time he had seen her, had produced the odd remark sour with racist intolerance.

She had had her sixteenth birthday in the summer, when Conor had given her — the foolish lad — the one object of real value he had ever unearthed with his metal detector, a sixteenth-century copper seal. He had had it, more expensively than he ought to have afforded, mounted on a gold chain, and she had worn it round her neck.

So she was involved in drugs, if only on the edges and over E tablets, which half a million stupid youngsters up and down the country took every weekend at discos and raves. But was she still? Would she have been on a buying expedition to Sandymount on Monday, if only as a hanger-on to some more adventurous boy? With Conor, surely, as a hanger-on at yet another remove, now keeping stum to protect her?

The knight errant. He felt a rush of warmth bringing tears, once more, to his eyes.

But no time for sentiment. The knight errant at this moment sitting opposite Dragon Verney feeling the hot fire of relentless questioning scalding his very skin. Perhaps even causing him to confess to something he had not done.

Or . . . Or worse, to confess to what, after all, he had done.

Because, look at it whichever way you would, it was still possible that Conor, knowing nothing about drugs, had heard that Mrs Unwala was supposed to know where the Hampton Hoard was buried. Had he really then, motivated more by a will-o'-the-wisp desire for quick glory than greed for gold, gone to the old professor and attempted to get him to say where his wife had located the Hoard? And then . . . ? Then met with adamant refusal had he lashed out with the first thing that came to hand? That ancient cricket bat.

It was still possible. Vicky's vague account of the time he had got back from school on Monday left it all open.

But at least now there was something to go on towards disproving that worst scenario. If Belinda Withrington was down in Sandymount on Monday evening, Conor's response when he had questioned him could be explained.

He swore.

If he was still on the case he would have had every right to send a detective who knew what he was about, someone like Jumbo Hastings, to the Withrington girl's house. Under the guise of wanting to find witnesses in Sandymount he could get permission to ask her some questions. Then almost as a certainty, if Conor had been there with her, she would say so.

But that line was forbidden to him now. He could not ask Jumbo or any other detective to do anything risking disciplinary action. So nothing for it but to go back to the nick and hope to bump into somebody who knows what's going on in the interview room. Somebody who will have the decency to tell me.

Unless it's all over. One way or the other.

At the station the person he bumped into was Di March, just coming out as he turned to go in. He would have passed her by with no more than a nod. But she called out from the top of the steps, the heavy double doors behind her still vibrating to a close. That intolerably loud voice, telling the whole dark street.

'Hi, guv. You're back then. Mr Verney's been looking for you. Tell you your little boy's been bailed. Let go about half an hour back. Only thing to do. Verney never had more than a sniff of a case. My view. Though, from all I hear, that doesn't mean he's giving up on your lad.'

His swamping sense of partial relief only just overrode fury at this high-handed treatment of himself and even of Superintendent Verney.

'Thanks for telling me,' he said, hurrying up the steps to give her less of an opportunity to trumpet out his concerns to the whole world. 'And do you happen to know where Conor is now?'

'Gone back to the place his mother shares with that Jack-the-Lad lover of hers, I imagine.'

So much for keeping his private life private. But, no doubt, she's right about where Conor is. Where else could he go?

Once more he gave the tinny goblin door knocker a vigorous shaking. It brought no response, although there was light behind the curtains of the room next to the door.

Standing there in the cold — another wave of fog seemed to be creeping in from the sea — the last time he had tattooed away at that silly little goblin came vividly back to him. Only a few hours after the murder had been discovered. Before he knew that the small huddled body with its head under a corner of that fallen bookcase was that of Professor Edul Unwala, Nobel Prize winner. At the time he had been stealing a few minutes from the investigation to make sure, on Vicky's adamant instructions, that Conor was at home, had eaten his tea, was doing the work he had been set.

Innocent Conor. Then. Guilty of no worse a crime than not regularly going straight back after school. Innocent Conor now, innocent of killing Professor Unwala? Evidently Verney at least had doubts. Otherwise he would have freed him, not bailed him.

And me, do I have doubts now? Am I now as convinced of Conor's innocence as I was when I set out to see that dusty raven at Harrison? Am I as convinced of his guilt as I was when I went hotfoot to th and poured out all my f   and suspicions?

The door in front of   utiously opening saved him from h   ng to answer.

It was Conor, just as it had been on Tuesday afternoon. Myself when young. That damned long Harrison Academy black jacket and the grey trousers. But tonight no white trainers, size seven, on his feet. Instead a pair of down-at-heel red leather slippers.

'Looking at the footwear, Dad? They took my trainers off me when I said they were the ones I wore all the time.'

Another wave of gratitude. Conor's survived. Or it seems he has. On an even keel, able to talk about his time down at the nick. God knows what internal damage there may

178

be though, surfacing God knows when later on. When he's taking his exams at the end of next academic year? Hoping he'll do well enough to get into Cambridge, go on to receive one day — there's irony — the Nobel Prize I jokingly forecast for him just before I realized why the name Unwala meant something? Or internal damage surfacing time and again while, the blackest outlook, he's serving life for murder?

He blinked and recovered himself.

'Can I come in? Tell me about it all. I'm on the case, of course. Don't know anything about what's been happening. And then I owe you an apology. Did Mr Verney tell you who put them on to you in the first place?'

'It sort of leaked out, yeah. But no hard feelings. I can see why you thought what you did.'

Like father, like son. Well, if I'm always accused of seeing both sides, I'm happy actually that my son's inherited that. Yes, by God, I am. Soft as a duck's arse, or not soft as a duck's arse, I think I'm right. And Conor's right too.

In the narrow hallway Conor murmured in his ear.

'You'll get a rocket from Mum, you know.'

'Expected. And prepared for.'

But no amount of preparation, and in point of fact he had not felt able to do much, would have readied him for the assault that met him as soon as he stepped into the cramped sitting room.

'You. I said it would be. Conor, go up to your room. Mike, I think you'd better step into the kitchen. You can peel the bloody potatoes, for once in your life.'

The two of them slunk out. As if retreating from a battlefield, soon to be blood-boltered, corpse-strewn.

'I don't know how you've got the fucking cheek to show yourself here.'

He stood for a moment dumbstruck.

'But — But listen, Vicky,' he brought out at last. 'Conor is my son too, you know.'

'Oh, yes. Your son, and you go telling that filthy pig Verney he's committed a murder. That your son has hit some old man on the head and then tried to hide his crime by hauling a bookcase on top of him. And you have the gall to stand there and say "He's my son". Your son. Christ, there ought to be a court order keeping you away from him for the rest of your life. If anything's ever abuse, it's what you did to Conor today.'

He tried to halt the onrush.

'Look, I know what I did may seem bad enough. But try to think of it from my point of —'

'Your point of view. Here we go again. Always has to be another way of looking at something. Christ, if you were lying in front of an oncoming train, you'd start worrying about what the engine driver was going to feel. You sicken me. You really do. You get some fantastic notion in your head that your son's gone down to some house in Sandymount and bashed to death a poor helpless old man, as if that's in any way likely, and you go rushing off to get your superior officers to harass the wretched boy till he doesn't know whether he's on his head or his heels.'

'Did . . . Did Verney harass him that much? Did you get a solicitor there? What happened in the interview? I know nothing. Nothing about my own son in a situation like that.'

'Well, what do you think happened? That pig bullied and shouted, and completely ignored the stupid solicitor we got given, and Conor went whiter and whiter till he could hardly get out any answer at all. And I suppose you're going to say your precious Mr Verney was only doing his duty? And it was quite fair of him to reduce your son almost to tears?'

'It was that bad?'

'Of course it was. You should have thought of that before you denounced Conor like a bloody informer under the Nazis. But oh, no. No, you had to go and betray the poor boy when what you ought to have been doing was getting him out of the country as fast as his legs would carry him.'

'But — But, listen, Vicky, why should I try to get him out of the country — as if I even possibly could — when, as you say, the boy's done nothing?'

'Done nothing? Is that what you're going to claim now? Your son has only killed a defenseless old man. And you say that's nothing. You disgust me, Phil Benholme. Disgust me more than I ever thought possible.'

He stood looking at her, blinking in bemusement. But before she caught her breath again, he managed to jerk in a question.

'Let me get this straight. Do you know Conor did it after all? Did he say something to you after he was let out on bail? My God, how could you have pretended to believe he did nothing if that's what he's said to you?'

'Oh, don't be more stupid than you can

help. Of course, he hasn't come running to Mummy saying *Sorry, sorry, I didn't mean to break your pretty necklace.* But that doesn't mean he didn't go to that house in Sandymount. Your Mr Verney seemed to be getting near the truth when he looked over what they'd taken from Conor's pockets and found that seal thing he dug up once with his detector. He accused him then of wanting to find the secret of the Hampton Hoard and going too far in trying to get it out of that pathetic old man. And I thought — Conor was getting even more upset than before — that he was going to tear it out of him at last.'

'But he didn't?'

'Of course he didn't. Do you think Conor would be here, gulping down a huge tea, if he'd confessed to doing that? I thought you at least knew about how the police work.'

Another jibe to be ignored.

'But what you're saying is, although Mr Verney's let Conor out on police bail, he's still convinced he's got the right person? And you're saying that you believe he has, too?'

'Well, he went on about having Conor in again after what he called *further inquiries.* So he plainly believes Conor's guilty. And if he is, whose fault is it? Whose fault is it that the boy doesn't know enough of right from wrong that he can go and do a thing like that?'

For an instant he wanted to shout at her that not ten minutes earlier she had been swearing black and blue that Conor was innocent. But he still had enough cool left to know that would get nobody anywhere.

'How can you say,' he began again in what he hoped was a reasonable tone, 'that Conor doesn't know right from wrong? What other instances make that even slightly likely? Is Conor an habitual liar? Does he steal? Does he bully kids weaker than himself? You know he doesn't.'

'And does he murder old men who get in his way? Do you know for certain that he doesn't do that? All right, in your eyes he's a little angel. But even you must admit the boy's got a really vicious temper when he does break out.'

A temper. Yes, Conor has that, though I'd dispute *really vicious*. So could he have . . . If for some almost unimaginable reason he had allowed himself to try to get the secret of the Hampton Hoard out of Professor Unwala would he, if the old man stood up to him, have altogether lost his temper? Can I really be sure then that he would have been able to control himself?

184

Well, no. No, I must admit it. I can't be sure. I can't. No one can say that about anyone.

'Yes. Well, I agree Conor's got a temper, a pretty violent temper sometimes. Who hasn't? Only one person in a thousand. In ten or twenty thousand, I dare say. But just because in the past on the odd occasion Conor's thrown an utter wobbly, it doesn't mean he killed Professor Unwala. He isn't capable of murder. He isn't.'

'Oh, isn't he? If he is — and, Christ, I can't swear that he isn't — then do you know why he is?'

What is this?

'Why should I know why?'

Her eyes gleamed yet more ferociously.

'Because of the way you've brought the boy up, Phil See-all-Sides Benholme. Because of the way you've always overruled me when I wanted you to punish him. The way you always said *Oh, I can see why he did it. It isn't the boy's fault. I know just how he feels.* When what he should have been feeling was the back of your hand. But you're just too bloody weak to do what you have to.'

Am I? Was I? Is she right, rage or no rage?

He stood there in the middle of the little

overheated room with its bulging, chintz-covered armchairs and asked himself if, never mind Vicky's shrieking and snarling, Conor had become capable of murder because all of his life he had been allowed too much of his own way.

And he could not make up his mind.

Chapter Twelve

He drove very slowly back from Frogs Lane to the house on the other side of town that he had shared for so long with Vicky. The house where Conor had been born, had been brought up over fifteen busy years. As he put his key in the door, from the estuary in the quiet of the night there came one last, long foghorn call, muffled and mournful.

But how well in those fifteen years had Conor been brought up?

The question he had asked himself so forcefully in the wake of Vicky's accusation had thumped away in his head, unanswered, unanswerable, all the while he had pushed onwards through the thickening fog. It thumped away still as he peered indifferently into the fridge, saw the four cold chipolatas congealed in whitish grease he had left on an old green saucer, all that remained of a wedding-present breakfast set for two. With a couple of slices from a stalish loaf they would do as supper. Thank God there was beer.

Setting down his glass tankard — another wedding present, he thought wryly, and again the only one of a set of four that had escaped Vicky's high rate of breakages, he stared straight ahead for a moment and then spoke aloud in the chill emptiness of the kitchen.

'Right. Get it sorted. Are you, Phil Benholme, responsible for your son committing murder because you let him get away with too much over the years?'

But at the other side of the pale grey plastic-topped kitchen table there was no Phil Benholme under interrogation. There was no shiny green interview-room table between these two Phil Benholmes, only the one he had known for so long, with the chip in its grey surface that had been there for five years or more, its painted legs scuffed and scarred from little Conor's kicking. A mute witness of family life. No way, sitting at it here, of getting any clear-cut yes or no to the obsessive question.

Getting up and putting plate and drained tankard into the sink, he thought that in any case it all depended on whether it was true that Conor was the person who had brought that cricket bat swinging down on to Professor Unwala's frail, white-haired skull. If the boy was a murderer, and boys as young as Conor had killed in circumstances as hard at first sight to credit, then perhaps he himself did have a grave charge to answer. And never mind that it had been put by Vicky in her typical no-holds-barred extravagant way. If, though, Conor had not killed Professor Unwala, but was simply protecting his Belinda, or his friend Alec Gaffney or some other mate, from getting into trouble over buying Ecstasy, then his upbringing hardly came into it. Or if it did, it was a credit to the way he had been brought up that he would go so far to protect a friend.

But could Conor go on fighting on that friend's behalf — if he was not in fact fighting to protect himself — hour after hour in the interview room, even day after day? For how long could he go on taking the sort of battering Verney had already given him, even if he was guiltless?

Then, suddenly, he thought he saw a reason for believing what he hardly dared believe, that Conor was not guilty. It was not the sort of reason you could very well put up as evidence in court, however brilliant a defence lawyer you were. But to him it had the ring of conviction.

It was the copper seal Conor had unearthed.

Six months ago Conor had gone to more expense than he could really manage to have that seal, his most precious find, mounted on its gold chain to give to Belinda for her birthday. The momentary thought of Belinda, as he had tried just a few moments ago to get the whole business straight in his head, had brought back to him now what Vicky had said in the heat of their row. *Your Mr Verney seemed to be getting near the truth when he looked over what they had taken from Conor's pockets and found that seal thing.*

Perhaps Verney had indeed been getting near the truth, he thought. The truth, not of Conor's guilt, but the truth of why he was refusing to say what he was doing in Sandymount. That seal had belonged to Belinda. After her birthday she had gone about perpetually wearing it. He could see it clearly now on its thin gold chain on the neat white blouse of her Harrison Academy girls' uniform, though in fact she had always been quick to discard white blouse, grey skirt and long black jacket in favour of jeans and breasts-enhancing T-shirt. So how did the seal come to be in Conor's pocket when he had been brought in to the Custody Suite and submitted to Sergeant Spage's rule-bound procedures? Answer, surely, because Belinda had returned it. And that very day. Otherwise Conor would have restored it to its place in his box of other treasure-hunting finds. Correction: detectorist finds.

So — surely this must be the truth — down in Sandymount on Monday evening for some reason, perhaps because of a disagreement about drugs, Conor and Belinda had quarrelled. And she had given the seal back to him, flung it at him probably. So was it likely that Conor would then have gone straight to Professor Unwala's to try and find out where the Hampton Hoard was buried? With his mind, as it must have been, in turmoil? Never in a million years.

But now . . . Now the still-loyal fellow, the silly fellow, the splendid fellow, was trying nevertheless to protect Belinda. But to protect her from what? Plainly from something more serious than, as had seemed likely when he had first heard she was involved in the drugs scene, attempting to buy a few Ecstasy tablets?

If the girl had been down in Sandymount simply to buy Ecstasy, would Conor have endured and endured Verney's interrogation to protect her? No. What would be the worst that could happen if she was found to have possessed a few tablets, even to have sold some on? Nothing surely to make it vital even for a misguided knight errant to go on and on lying for her.

So . . .

So Belinda Withrington could well be involved, directly or indirectly, in Professor Unwala's death. And Conor could be no more than a witness to whatever discussions there had been beforehand.

But, he thought with a sudden access of irony, none of all this was going to be accepted as proof, either by Verney, or, supervising the case from Headquarters, by Detective Chief Superintendent Fothergill, or by any lawyer in the Crown Prosecution Service. And, true enough, all this supposition was the sort of airy tower that might at any moment be brought to nothing by one solid fact telling in the opposite direction.

He could not, either, however much he himself felt this was convincing, go to Verney and try to make him see the real implications. Off the case. He was off the case. Properly so, if his own son truly was the prime suspect.

So tomorrow or the next day, if the further inquiries he had spoken about turned up whatever extra evidence Verney was hoping, Conor would have to face another session

on the wrong side of the table in the interview room. And, even if he had had nothing
to do with the actual killing, it would be a
nerve-shattering experience for him. All
right, he had seemed, earlier at the cottage
door, to be very much on an even keel. But
that was like him. He never let his inner
fears show. Like son, like father. You could
only get to have a hard enough exterior to
be a working detective by making yourself
look hard. By not letting the doubts and the
fears show.

Well, letting the doubts show a little. You
didn't get labelled soft as a duck's arse if
you never let your second thoughts show.
And, by God, no harm in letting others see
that you believed things weren't always un-
alterably black and white. And that you were
willing to act on that. But the fears were
better thrust down. As no doubt Conor had
thrust his down when Verney's pressure was
for the moment off.

Yet the boy had not been able to push
away those fears all the time. Hadn't Vicky
described him as going whiter and whiter
as Verney had banged and battered on?

And I don't think she was exaggerating
there.

So how will Conor stand up to a new
bout of it? Verney, the tank, grinding ever

forwards to his objective, reality or mirage.

God knows.

Go to bed. Only thing to do.

A night of broken sleep. Muzzy dreams where Verney loomed nightmare-like, half man, half gun-swivelling battle tank, interrogating remorselessly sometimes himself, sometimes Conor.

Come on, lad. There's no point in you sitting there saying nothing. You know we're going to get to the truth sooner or later, don't you? Now, why not save yourself and your mother here a lot of needless anxiety? Eh? Oh? Now, come on, just tell me all about it.

Come on now, Benholme, we know what the truth is. Why not just face up to it? You're soft as a duck's arse. Isn't that what it is? Soft as a duck's arse. Now why not just admit it. Get it off your chest.

Look, lad, don't piss me about. Do you think I've got nothing better to do than sit here listening to you telling fairy tales? You were down in Sandymount. We know that. And you went into that house in Percival Road. Yes?

It's you that's to blame, Benholme. It's you who brought about this whole appalling mess. Now, there's only one thing for you to do. Cough to it, Benholme. Admit it. You're guilty.

Guilty as all hell. So, come on, say it. Admit it. Admit it.

You thought of yourself as the great archaeologist, isn't that it, lad? Saw your name in the papers. Bit of instant fame. Encouraged, of course, by that father of yours. Spoiling you the way he always has. So you got this idea you could get your fame the easy way. But he wouldn't talk, would he, the old gent? And then you killed him? You picked up that cricket bat and you killed him.

You killed him, Benholme. You killed your own son. You shopped him, and, worse, worse, worse, you made him the nasty little murderer he is. You. You. It was you.

Fighting off a dull headache in the morning, as he came into the station and passed the Muster Room, still the Incident Room, he forced himself to quicken his pace so as to avoid any hint of lurking there to find out what was happening inside. But he could not help hearing Di March's voice through the closed doors.

'What's the point, for Christ's sake? Trying to trace everywhere that little bleeder went? Claiming he was no nearer than that corner shop? For God's sake, we know he did it. Why the hell should I go checking

195

an alibi any fool can see is fake? If I had the case I'd get the cough all right. Across the interview-room table.'

He stood rooted to the brown vinyl floor of the corridor. It was only too plain she was talking about Conor, *that little bleeder.* Conor under questioning yesterday must have said he had been at the shop where fat Mrs Damberry worked. Presumably when that made it more or less impossible for him to have been in number twelve at the time of the *You black bastard* yell.

But why had Conor been able to claim he was at the shop then? Something surely must have happened there for him definitely to remember. The row he had with Belinda? Would that have been the very spot where she had flung the copper seal he had given her to the pavement, as they had stood in the fog arguing, say, about buying Ecstasy? And then, black with depression, had he started straight off for Frogs Lane?

It could be. Or he may have been sure about the place for a hundred other reasons. But the point was that he had seen this as at least a partial alibi for himself, presumably one he believed he could put forward without compromising Belinda. Or whichever of his other friends he was protecting.

If he was. If all this isn't my mere deluded hopefulness.

And Verney, either because he wants by disproving this finally to break down his sullen young suspect, or because — give him credit — he's genuinely prepared to look for what he can in Conor's favour, has tasked various detectives with tracing the route Conor has claimed he took. So March is being sent to confirm or otherwise what Conor said about the corner shop.

March busy swearing black and blue she believes Conor's a killer. March, who'll undertake her task with contemptuous briskness, mind made up.

So . . .

He broke out of his statue-still trance and hurried back to where he had just left his car.

He did not have to sit in it long before he saw March come stamping out; making for her own bright red little roadster. Just like her herself. As soon as she roared away he set off in pursuit.

In the fog he did not drive at as much of a pace as March set. But, as he expected, when he came to Percival Road he saw the red roadster parked outside the goods-crammed corner shop. He drove on past, confident of not being spotted inside his car with the fog thick all around, and came to a halt some fifty yards along. Then he walked quickly back.

Approaching with care, he found once again he had reason to bless March's crowd-quelling voice. She was evidently addressing, not big, garrulous Mrs Damberry, but the shop owner.

'And that's all you saw, Mr Patel? This boy in that school uniform, black jacket, that horrible yellow and green striped tie, knocking over your National Lottery board outside?'

Softly spoken reply inaudible from his place of observation just round the corner. But March, once more, ringing out what she had to say.

'And you can't describe him any better than that? He might have been any boy from Harrison Academy, yes? Or some other boy who just happened to be wearing some sort of black coat? Right?'

He had edged nearer the propped-open shop door, and Mr Patel's answer came more audibly.

'No, no, madam. I am well knowing which boy it was.'

'Oh, you are, are you? And why are you so sure all of a sudden? You may have to give evidence in court, you know. You'd better be certain of your facts.'

'Oh, madam, madam, I am not at all wishing . . .'

But now, booming almost as loudly as March, Mrs Damberry evidently had a contribution to make.

'Lady, we all knowing that boy. He coming in once, twice a week these days. He buying a Coke. Not like those friend of he always comin' in, wanting half-whisky.'

'Never mind all the Cokes and whiskies. Would you be willing to go into the witness box and swear on the Bible you're telling the truth when you identify this boy as having been outside this shop, knocking over that National Lottery ad?'

'Holy Bible jus' right for Marguerite Damberry. Yes, ma'am. I ready to swear I know that boy. Don't know he name for sure, but I knowing his dad.'

'His dad? What is it you're trying to tell me now?'

'You was in here Tuesday morning, right?'

'Yes, of course I was. Making inquiries in connection with the murder in the house along the road.'

'Well, you was with a gennelman, yes? Inspector? Big Chief Inspector he saying?'

'Detective Chief Inspector Benholme, if

that's got anything to do with anything.'

'Lady, it certain sure has. He that boy father, yes? Like as two buttons on same dress.'

'Well, yes. Yes, you're right, as a matter of fact. The boy I'm asking about is in fact DCI Benholme's son.'

'Well then, lady. He outside here Monday evenin'.'

'All right, so he was. But at what time? Are you going to tell me you looked at that clock there the moment he knocked over that board? And in any case the damn thing's wrong, you know. Five minutes out, more.'

'Madam, madam,' the owner of the maligned clock stepped in now, his voice rising in a defensive wail. 'Clock is kept five minutes slow always. So we are never selling alcoholic liquors before correct hour.'

'Five minutes slow or five minutes fast,' March banged out. 'If nobody looked at the clock when the boy was outside here, if he was here at all, then nobody can say what time it was.'

'But, madam, I am able. You see, I was not going out to pick up sign — Lottery people are saying same must be always on full display — because I was having to switch on telly.'

'Oh, come on. You could have switched on your TV at any time.'

'No, no, madam. I am switching on for my very very aged mother to be watching *Neighbours*. She is altogether bedridden, and same is her lifeline only.'

From his place of concealment he could actually hear the gigantic sigh March heaved.

'All right, let's get this straight. A boy that Mrs Damberry here will swear to being Conor Benholme knocked down the lottery sign outside this shop just before *Neighbours* began at — what is it? — five-thirty-five last Monday? Is that it?'

Mrs Damberry entered the fray once more.

'That darn well it. Conor Benholme, if that he name, come running, running past here just after it gone half past five, Monday, knocked over that sign, one big metal crash, and then run off, hard as he can go.'

'Ran off, yes. But in which direction? Along Percival Road, wasn't it?'

'No, ma'am. He run along Lancelot Road, right bang in other direction.'

'Lancelot Road? You're not making that up? You've got some interest in the boy?'

'Ma'am, I damn well ain't. He a nice boy all right, not like that big tall friend of he or that girl no better than should be who come in with him some time. But Marguerite Damberry always tell truth, and truth she telling now. Lancelot Road it was. Lancelot Road fast as he can run.'

'Well, if that's your story . . .'

March patently trying to reconcile her made-up mind with the given facts.

Hastily he swung round and walked stealthily away till he was out of sight in the swirling fog.

Chapter Thirteen

He stood there beside his car, shivering in the fog. But inwardly he felt a warm glow. All right, the fact that Conor had run off in the opposite direction from Professor Unwala's house at twenty-five to six, *Neighbours* soap time, did not necessarily mean he could not have doubled back and been inside the house half an hour later when Mrs Ahmed had heard the *black bastard* yell. But it was a strong indication he really had had no intention of going there.

In fact, the picture of what Conor had most probably done that late afternoon and early evening was becoming clearer. Yes, he had gone to Sandymount. Was it because Belinda Withrington was going there, probably to buy Ecstasy? If it was, had Conor gone to stop her? Or was he, poor boy, caught in that complicated, on-off state of falling out of love still just trailing round wherever she went? Perhaps Conor's redhead friend Alec Gaffney had been there too. Could he be the boy Belinda had switched to?

Then — the evidence of the copper seal — Conor and Belinda had in all probability had a blazing row. Over love? No, over Ecstasy, more likely. And then Conor had run off blindly, furiously. Wheeling round the corner by the shop, with tears in his eyes perhaps, he had crashed into that clanging metal National Lottery sign, and, heedless in his misery about setting it up again, had plunged off, away along Lancelot Road. Firm evidence of Mrs Damberry.

And Lancelot Road was at least the start of his way out to Frogs Lane.

Now if any of the other detectives Verney has tasked — if he has sent anyone out — finds evidence for Conor being at any point on the route between Lancelot Road and Frogs Lane, he'll definitely be off the hook.

Who will be on it?

Not my business.

Oh, but, yes. Yes, it could very soon be my business again. If Conor is proved to have had nothing to do with the murder, then there's no reason why I should be off the case. And, by God, I'll do my utmost to get back on it again. It is very much my business. And I'll bloody well see it through.

Yet sitting that afternoon actually dealing with some of the paperwork — clearing the decks: expenses claims due to be checked tomorrow — it still came as a sharp surprise when the phone shrilled and Verney spoke.

'Mr Benholme, come down to the Incident Room, will you? There's work here you should be doing.'

Work in the Incident Room I should be doing? Then Conor's in the clear. Must be. Verney did get Conor's route to Frogs Lane checked. Conor's no longer the prime suspect. No longer any suspect at all.

He felt himself almost melting into jelly with relief.

For two whole minutes, more, he simply sat where he was, unable to think, unable even to move. The nightmare over. Over, over, over.

And typical Verney, he thought when he began to come to himself, to ring me with that terse, uncommunicative message. The encased hard man. Wouldn't, as they say, give away the drips from his own nose. Never thinking, unless forced to confronting a suspect of some sort, what anybody else might be feeling. Typical of him not to have let it enter his head what my thoughts might be, hearing that my son was no longer considered a murder suspect. Typical not to think of giving me any details of just what has in the end cleared Conor. I suppose he's had the decency to tell Vicky, though I could believe it of him that it's not occurred to him.

No, all I get is that curt *There's work here you should be doing.* And back, as far as Verney's concerned, exactly to the situation as it was before. To a murder inquiry with, as yet, little sight of an answer.

But an inquiry that's once again my business. I'm on the case again.

And I'd better not keep Verney waiting one minute more.

The Incident Room, when he pushed open its no longer forbidden doors, looked little different from when he had suggested to the Gill that the black-coated figure asthmatic Mr Jones had seen in the fog might be, not his own son as he had secretly feared, but some senior Harrison Academy boy.

Then, when the Gill accepted my reason for setting off on my own to check out Harrison boys, it had been off instead to see if Vicky could give Conor an alibi. Then that row when she failed to be precise enough. Bloody ironic that it turns out

Conor actually got back to the cottage altogether early enough. And I never came into the Incident Room here again after that. Sitting in the car, out of range of Vicky's anger trying to think whether or not I believed Conor was guilty, and then suddenly realizing I'd only just be in time for the press conference. In the wake of that, fearing the worst, seeking the worst even, going to the Gill and telling him everything. Then, guillotine descending, *Off the case.*

He would have been hard put to it to say precisely how he had imagined the Incident Room would have changed in his absence. Rationally he knew that nothing would be essentially different. Yet he felt that Conor's time being questioned and the thoughts and, yes, hopes of those in the room while that was going on would have left some physical impression.

But, bar the files on the big central table being the bulkier for some twenty-four hours of reports coming in and checked actions being filed, the place looked almost exactly as it had before. The computer screens ranked along their wall were glowing as greyly as ever, though fewer of them were manned. The remains of half-eaten snacks on paper plates littered the place as previously, perhaps a little more numerously.

The big cardboard files in front of Jumbo Hastings may have been some degrees fatter, but otherwise looked unchanged. Only the ashtrays fuller with sharp-smelling stubbed-out ends.

The chair at the table at the top of the room was now, of course, Verney's since he had chosen to conduct a hands-on operation. But it looked almost as it had done when he himself had last got up from it. Its in-basket almost as full, its out-basket a little fuller. There were perhaps fewer pads of rough paper on it, and more chewed pencils. The waste bin was, however, just as full of crushed plastic tea and coffee beakers. But that was all.

Verney, as he presented himself to him, leant closely enough forwards for what he said not to be overheard.

'Take over the day-to-day now, Phil, I want to get back to my own office. But keep me informed. Every detail. Every detail that matters.'

Again, the barest word. But now it was *Phil*. Back, though no other indication had emerged, to complete confidence. Still, that was Verney's style. And it would be easy enough, going through all the files to bring himself up to date, to see what precisely it had been that had finally cleared Conor.

'Yes, sir,' he answered, with a hidden bound of pleasure. 'Will do.'

But, as soon as Verney had gone, he picked up the phone and rang the Frogs Lane cottage. If Verney really had neglected to tell Vicky that Conor was no longer a suspect and could go back to school rather than sit waiting to be called in for another questioning session, then he had better make sure Conor knew.

However, at the far end the phone rang and rang and was never picked up.

OK, down to work.

'Sergeant,' he called out to Jumbo, who from the moment he had come in had given out, for all his scrupulously turned back, a warm gust of welcome. 'Let's have the latest files. I've got catching up to do.'

Jumbo brought across a whole armful of bulky clip-in files and dumped them with a loud smack on the table.

'All in chronological, boss,' he said. 'You shouldn't have much trouble picking up. I'd start this one from the end, though, I were you. Three places where we found witnesses to young Conor's trek home.'

'Jumbo. Thanks.'

And one quick flip-through confirmed it all.

'Jumbo,' he said, 'd'you happen to know

if Vicky's been told that Conor's totally in the clear now?'

'Can't say I do. Certainly Mr Verney never asked me to tell her. Wouldn't put it past him never to have thought. He's not exactly one to consider other people.'

'No. No, I suppose he's not.'

Well, I know damn well he's not. So has Vicky, out there with Conor, decided perhaps to get him out of the way in case he's summoned back for another interview? Is that why the phone was unanswered?

But, on the other hand, I may be maligning Verney. He may have phoned Vicky with the good news, and Conor's gone back to Harrison. And Vicky's gone . . . shopping? To the hairdresser? Whatever.

So, he thought, as he began systematically to go through the new stuff in the files, if Conor's totally out of the frame — how could I ever have thought . . . ? — then who is in it? Who? One of the bad lads we have on our lists? Two of the most notorious had been brought in for questioning. But none of the doorstepping inquiries had yielded anything even a little hopeful.

Then, as he let the last of the files flop down in front of him, like an obedient genie rubbed from a lamp the shadow of a notion flicked across his mind. He went quickly back through the file detailing Conor's walk from the shop in Sandymount out to Frogs Lane and found Di March's filled-in Action sheet.

It was, he noted as he went through it again, very competently done. Whatever prejudice March had had when she was on her way to the shop had been thoroughly disposed of by the facts she had gathered there. And she had fully reported them.

But there was, as he had been faintly aware of from his earlier quick glance, one omission. It had no direct bearing on the action March had been tasked with, and so the gap was perfectly reasonable. But the very absence was putting more and more strongly into his mind what it was that he had overheard, back flattened against the wall just round the corner from the shop's open door.

It was something Mrs Damberry had said. Or rather had sung out in vigorous contradiction. *Not like those friends of he.*

He could hear her voice now.

So, regular customers at the shop, besides Conor buying Cokes, were friends of Conor's. Buying, if they were let, half-bottles of whisky. As well as the Ecstasy they got in all probability elsewhere in Sandymount before most weekends or when there was a party somewhere. But whisky and Ecstasy tablets don't come cheap. All right, a top dentist like Belinda's father must be pretty well off, and Alec's father, the estate agent, certainly won't be short of a penny. But there's surely a limit to the amount of spending money either of them will let their kids have. So, isn't it likely the two youngsters, regularly swanning about down in Sandymount, would have heard, like Conor, of the famous Hampton Hoard? Perhaps even heard Conor himself mention it.

So, what if the two of them had hatched a plan to get the location of the Hoard out of old Professor Unwala? Was Alec Gaffney, then, the black-coated figure breathless Mr Jones had seen lurking in Percival Road? Had it been Alec who had at last yelled out, in a falsetto of baulked rage, *You black bastard?* Swung that cricket bat, hauled the bookcase over in a feeble attempt to make the death look like an accident? And had then gone on to escape by way of the garden? To vomit there? Likely enough for a first-time killer, still a teenager. And in scrambling over that tall concrete fence, had left a footmark? But wait. Alec Gaffney's tall, a good six foot. Would he really have size seven feet?

Except for this last circumstance, the facts

fitted well enough for all that they by no means pointed to a clearcut culprit. But worth going to Verney — *Keep me informed. Every detail* — and suggesting that, if the Gaffney boy's presence in Sandymount on Monday evening could be confirmed, then a few informal words with him might produce enough to give us our much-needed firm new lead.

Yes.

Ten minutes later he was driving once more through the still-persistent fog down to Sandymount and the corner shop. But this time no need to hover outside.

'Mrs Damberry, good afternoon. You remember me, Detective Chief Inspector Benholme?'

He was answered with a hugely beaming smile.

'Marguerite Damberry jus' only talking 'bout you this morning. You an' that good-lookin' son of you.'

He smiled back, impossible not to.

'As a matter of fact,' he said, 'I know you were. It's in the police files. But no need to let that worry you. What you told Detective Sergeant March this morning helped to get my lad out of a bit of a hole he'd foolishly dug himself into.'

'Foolish? No, sir. That boy ain't foolish.

He got he head good an' screwed on he shoulders. Not like some of he friends.'

He pounced at this.

'Well, it's about his friends that I've come to see you. The point is we're anxious to get hold of as many people as possible, witnesses, who were round about here at the time Mr Unwala was killed.'

Mrs Damberry heaved an immense sigh.

'That poor old man. I misses him. I truly do.'

'I'm sure you do. And if I can find anybody who was around that evening, and who may have seen something they paid no particular attention to at the time, I may be all the nearer to finding who was responsible for his murder.'

'If Marguerite Damberry can help she'd tell you one hundred name. But she can't. She just didn't see no one that night, it so foggy.'

'No one at all, Mrs Damberry? I mean, besides my boy knocking your lottery sign flying, did any others from his school come into the shop by any chance? Or did you see any of them outside? In those long black jackets and with those stripy yellow and green ties?'

'Don't talk to me 'bout black jackets, stripe ties. That hussy off with hers, I dare say, almost before bell rung for end of school. I never see her in no black jacket, like I ought when she with her schoolfriends.'

Well, not a Harrison Academy routine to ring an end-of-school bell. But I know what she means about Belinda. And I'm not surprised to hear it. If it really is Belinda Withrington she's talking about. But is it?

'That's the blonde girl you may have seen with my son in the past? Called Belinda?'

'That be her. Belinda. What sort of name is that? I never heard of no Belinda, till I hear of that hussy.'

'So you know her? Know her by sight? And was she by any chance in the shop here on Monday evening?'

'She was. And that tall young feller with white face, red, red hair. Trying to buy whisky they was. Giving out and pretending he old enough. But Marguerite Damberry know better. And Mr Patel he scared, scared of losing he licence. So not one drop was they getting.'

'You haven't ever happened to hear that tall young fellow's name?'

'No, sir. I ain't never. But I know he. He not a good boy for your son to be friend with.'

'Well, perhaps you're right. But, you

know, you have to let a boy like my Conor choose his own mates.'

'No, sir. That where, savin' you presence, you wrong. Marguerite Damberry won't never let her kids go 'bout with no riff-raff, no, sir.'

He felt a little miffed at the unexpected rebuke.

But, well, he said to himself, her circumstances are different. No doubt there's plenty of riff-raff about in Sandymount to keep your kids clear of, if you can. But back to inquiries at hand.

'Yes, well . . . Now about what you were telling me, about that girl Belinda and her redhead friend. What time was it they were in here? Think carefully, if you will. Don't be offended, but it's important I get the facts exactly right.'

'You want exac' facts. You gone get 'em. Them two was in here trying to buy themselves one half-bottle White Horse jus' two, three minutes after that son of you was knocking down the lottery. He in one terrible state 'bout something. That for certain. An' they two going out of here pretty quick, tail between they legs. 'Cept that hussy girl swearing dreadful an' saying she could go somewhere else. An' so she could. Only Mr Patel careful, careful who he sell spirit liquors to round here. This be bad, bad neighborhood, you know, Mr Detective. Even before they do that thing to poor old Mr Un.'

Right. I wanted exact facts. I've got them. Alec Gaffney was here in this shop, not two hundred yards from where Professor Unwala was murdered, and only half an hour beforehand.

So, it is possible . . .

Chapter Fourteen

Once again waiting outside the gates of Harrison Academy. Verney had felt that, though the Alec Gaffney theory was possible, it was no more than a theory and could get them no further unless there was some confirmation. So an informal word with Alec had seemed their best try. And where better than just outside his school? Would anything come of such a casual-seeming chat? Although Mrs Damberry had not been able to put a name to Alec, it was almost certain he had been near the murder scene at a time shortly before it had happened. But now, standing stamping his feet in the fog-chilled November dusk till four o'clock, he found he was filled with doubts.

Damn it, if it went against the grain to believe Conor was responsible, why should I now believe it of his friend, the same age or a bit more, the same background? Is it really likely he's a murderer? All very well for Mrs Damberry to call him *riff-raff*, but she can't be an infallible judge of character. Of course I know boys a good deal younger have killed old people in the course of a mugging. But I never really felt Conor would do such a thing. So why should I think it of Alec Gaffney?

And why must those damn ships out there keep sounding their foghorns in that way? Bloody gets on your nerves. Prehistoric monsters moving about out there in the fog, yearning for each other. Primitive forces.

Four o'clock. And suddenly tall Alec Gaffney there in the familiar milling exodus of chattering, laughing, occasionally lugubrious pupils, one of whom years before he had been himself. Poll of red hair easy to spot over the scores of other heads, perhaps in close chat with Conor, too short to be seen in the jostling crowd. Conor telling him all about being interrogated by Detective Superintendent Verney.

But not, if Conor was with him, also with Belinda. Not after the row that had resulted in Conor's copper seal being no longer in Belinda's possession.

Now, in a high-pitched wave of talking, arguing, joking, the first of them were out on the pavement.

And here's Alec at the gates.

No Conor beside him. Well, no particular

reason why he should be. Perhaps he's lingering until the tail-end of the procession. Perhaps, even, he's manoeuvring to chat up some new girl? Off with the old . . . Good for him, if it is that way.

But cut off young Alec. Take him aside, ask him a question or two. See where they lead.

'It's Alec Gaffney, isn't it? I think I've seen you about with my son, Conor. I'm Detective Chief Inspector Benholme.'

And at once the look of alarm.

It almost told him in one instant all he needed to know. Certainly half of it. Plainly this red-headed beanpole of a boy, pale freckledy face, big beak-like nose, had something to hide. Something of which he was, surely, ashamed. Something — is it? — he hopes and hopes no police officer will ever get to hear about.

But is it that he entered the house in Percival Road and there battered to death old Professor Unwala? Not necessarily. He may simply be scared because he has in the pocket of his long black Harrison jacket, uncovered as always by any warmer outerwear, three or four Ecstasy tablets.

One thing. Size seven trainers? Quick glance down. And, yes, trainers. White, quite clean. And, hard to be sure, but Alec

Gaffney, however tall he is, has got very small feet for his height. Size seven, or seven and a half, to judge from my own eights, like Conor's small enough.

'I just wanted a word, Alec. Let's get out of the way of this mob.'

By placing himself to the boy's side and a little behind him he got him well clear of anyone overhearing. Around them a tall envelope of fog hovered, its droplets both catching and dissipating the light from a newly lit street lamp.

'Do you know where Conor is, actually?' he asked, as an unthreatening start. 'I thought he might be with you.'

The boy visibly relaxed.

'No. He didn't come into school today. I thought he —' He came to a halt.

Embarrassed, no doubt. On the point of saying *I thought he was being questioned by you police.* Something of that sort. Well, evidently Vicky's decided he can miss half a day's classes. Not go back till tomorrow. Fair enough. He's had a pasting at Verney's hands. He deserves a little peace and quiet. Odd, though, that he wasn't there when I phoned. But Vicky quite likely to have rushed off out with him somewhere when they heard he was no longer wanted at the station.

He experienced a pang of envy. Wasn't it a father's duty, a father's privilege, to reassure a son, one man to another, after an ordeal such as Conor had gone through?

'Well, never mind,' he said, with forced heartiness. 'I'll see Conor soon enough. But it's you I want a word with now.'

'Oh yes?'

A spark of defiance. Protective defiance? No more than the usual teenager's attitude to the police? Or a desperate attempt to stave off questions that could easily bring his life to ruin?

But, whatever its cause, it was going to do him little good. Easy enough to see the sort of thing going on just under the thin defiant layer, and to guess how it could crack. The merest touch of toughness would do the trick.

'Yes, I want a word or two. You've heard, of course, of the murder that took place down in Sandymount last Monday evening? Professor Unwala, the Nobel Prize winner?'

In the deceptive light as the street lamp fought with the fog he had more difficulty than he would have liked in seeing the boy's reaction.

'Yeah, everybody knows about that.'

But it sounded as if he was biting off the words of his reply, keeping them to the very minimum. In case something he said betrayed him?

'Well, we've had a report that someone, a man or a youth, wearing a black jacket, most likely Harrison Academy uniform, was seen waiting about — it was a foggy evening then, too — in the neighborhood of the house in Percival Road at the time. And we're trying to find who it was. To eliminate them from our inquiries. Or in case they saw something or someone that would be helpful to us.'

Plenty of opportunity there for the boy, if he was in Sandymount for some good reason, to say so.

'But why should you think that the person in a black jacket was me? It might not even have been anyone from Harrison.'

Again a rising note of defiance.

Time for a little embroidery.

'Ah, didn't I say? This person lurking there, lurking or whatever he was doing, has been described as tall and with red hair.'

Now there was a reaction plain to see even in the chancy light. A look of blank fear. And no answer.

'So, was it you, Alec? Did you have some reason, then, to be down in Sandymount that evening?'

'Conor. Conor told you I was.'

'Well, no, he didn't as a matter of fact. We had a description that fitted you from another source altogether. But tell me the truth now, what were you doing down there?'

'No.' He gulped. 'No, I wasn't there. I don't care who told you I was. They got it wrong. I was never there at all.'

A spate of denial that meant, surely, the exact opposite of what was said. Take the boy in now? He's certainly as much in the frame as ever Conor was. Guilt, guilt at least of some sort, written all over him. A single session with Verney, we'll find out just what the strength of it is.

But no. No, I'd like to talk to Verney first, see what he thinks. I could be wrong. See both sides of it. All right, the boy was pretty certainly near Percival Road on Monday evening. But he may only have been hoping to get some Ecstasy.

So just smooth him down so he won't try running.

'Well,' he said to the gangling figure he was sharing the glistening fog-encased envelope with, 'I'm happy to take your word for it. If you weren't there, you weren't there. And you can't help us. So I'll say goodnight. I expect I'll see you about with Conor sometime.'

Alec swung away, quickly as an object released by a spring. In a moment the fog and dark had swallowed him up.

He decided, before going to see Verney, to ring the Frogs Lane cottage again. If Verney really had not let Vicky know officially that Conor was no longer a suspect, he could hardly see how he could ask him directly whether or not he had contacted her. Altogether too much like criticizing a senior officer to his face.

But, once more, the phone at the other end rang and rang and was not picked up. He tried the number twice again in case he had been misrouted. Then he gave up.

After all, Vicky could have been officially informed and then had decided to take Conor out for a meal. Or to the cinema. Anywhere. Because — the thought only came wholly into his consciousness now — Conor, although he had seemed when he had let him into the cottage last night, to be very much as usual had perhaps been a little subdued. Was his mild joking then only a sign of inner unease? Had his time under Verney's tongue-lashing done more psychological damage than it appeared on the surface?

No doubt it had. No fifteen-year-old

could undergo that and not be affected. Deeply affected. So Vicky was probably — no, almost certainly — right to do all she could to take his mind off those long hours in the interview room, the chilling atmosphere of its harsh painted-brick walls, the daylight coming in only through an area of dull glass bricks, its bare, hard-surfaced green table, the recording machine whirring on and on.

Not that I blame Verney entirely for any harm Conor may have suffered. His duty to do what he did. Find out, if he could, who had killed, brutally killed, old Professor Unwala. And the circumstances at the time had clearly indicated Conor might be that killer. So any tough tactics to break him down in order.

Yet tough tactics perhaps not the only way of getting a confession. Don't I myself believe otherwise? Understanding the best way in the end. But there are detectives in plenty, successful detectives, with the opposite view. The no-holds-barred school.

So, if Conor isn't at home — *at home,* the words were still bitter — at the cottage, he isn't. What's more, if Vicky doesn't actually know Conor's off the hook, she may have gone out with him so as not to be there if the phone should ring and Verney want to question him once more. Again, a more or less reasonable thing to do.

Verney, though grudging as ever, agreed that Alec Gaffney should be left unquestioned for the time being.

'Dare say you're right, Phil. I don't see there's much point in having him in tonight. Don't want some bloody clever solicitor saying we used Gestapo tactics. No, tomorrow's Saturday, so he won't be at school. You go along to the house nice and early before the lad's had time to go gallivanting off, and we'll see what he's got to say for himself then.'

'Very good, sir.'

Ask now whether he's informed Vicky about Conor?

One look at Verney's solid, straightmouthed face — those hefty eyebrows and sombre eyes — made him realize that, however good the terms they now seemed to be on, suggesting he had not done what he should have was not a clever idea.

'I'll see you tomorrow then, sir, with the boy. About nine?'

'Very good, Mr Benholme.'

One more phone call to the cottage. Once again the distant bell ringing and ringing. Once more a mental parade of all the reasons why the cottage should be unoccupied.

He looked at his watch.

Not yet half past five. By six or shortly after, if what Vicky had said was true when he had been trying to find out exactly what time Conor had come in, loverboy Mike should be home. *Two minutes after he came in I was in the bedroom. On the bloody bed.* Then perhaps I'll find out what's been happening. Even if, when I ring, it turns out Conor and Vicky are back too. And Vicky on that bed. With Conor in the next room only too aware of what's going on between his mother and that sports-mad idiot. Who, thanks to my neglect of my wife in favour of police duties, does have some sort of right to be on the bed, trousers round under his bum.

But after sitting in the Incident Room riffling pointlessly through old witness statements, he still got no answer when, promptly at six, he rang once more. Wryly he told himself that by making the call on the dot, with the unacknowledged object of forestalling events on the bed, it served him right not to get a reply.

He sat then, not even flicking through the old witness statements, watching the second hand of his watch sweep slowly round and round till five past six had been reached.

Then he put through yet another call.

And at a quarter past six, another. And at twenty-past, yet one more.

What the hell has happened to the fellow, he asked himself. Why isn't he home by now? And where's Vicky? Where's she taken Conor? Are they really at the cinema? If they are, how long have they been there? When's it reasonable to expect them back?

Or have they, a new idea, contacted Mike at his work — what the hell is it he does? — and suggested he meet them somewhere in town for an early dinner? To celebrate? Well, Vicky would be well capable of feeling that Conor escaping Verney's clutches was reason to go out to celebrate. Lack of celebrations, and suddenly cancelled celebrations, had in the old days been one of the sharpest causes of her discontent.

Abruptly he stood up.

'Jumbo,' he said, 'are you on duty much longer?'

'Another hour, boss. Then old Arnold's coming in. Keep things going overnight, in so far as anything is going.'

'Right. Well, I'm off. If I'm wanted I won't be at home. I'm going out to Vicky's place, see how my lad is. The number's there, if you need it. OK?'

'OK, guv.'

But is it OK, he asked himself as, hurrying, he went out to the yard to find his car. Is it OK? Why do I feel it isn't?

The fog, sweeping in from the sea once more, made the drive out to Frogs Lane appallingly slow. Leaning forward over the wheel, eyes red with staring at the scarcely penetrable blanket in front of him, he cursed and swore. At times he could go no faster than a five-mile-an-hour crawl, and even when the fog seemed to lighten he could scarcely double that speed.

But at last he reached the cottage.

Dark. Not a light coming from the window beside the door. Not, as he felt his way up the path, even a chink of light from under the door.

Snickering with anxiety, he felt for the tinny goblin knocker and tap-tap-tapped a long tattoo with it. No answer.

Then the slightest of movements of the door under the feeble impact of the trumpery knocker alerted him. He put his hand flat on the door's surface and gently pushed. It swung open in front of him.

No one at home, and the door left unlocked? What on earth . . . ?

He reached around for a light switch, found it. The narrow entrance way told him nothing more. He pushed open the sitting-room door, already just ajar, and found the light switch in there.

The room seeming just as he had seen it when he was last at the cottage. When, he thought with a pang of sharp self-questioning, Vicky had so furiously accused him of ruining Conor by indulging him. The chintz-covered armchairs loomed hard against each other as before. The mantelpiece of bulky hacked-out stone stood over the little electric fire, as before, except that no orange glow was coming from its heater wires. The telephone, which he instinctively glanced at on the gateleg table, thinking how it must have rung and rung in the empty room when he had called and called again, was just where it had been before.

With, beside it, the spiral-bound message pad, fresh page uppermost. He strode across to see — he hardly knew why — what was written on it.

Yes. In Conor's unmistakable handwriting, using a ballpoint plainly on the edge of running out, just four words.

Mum. Sorry I can't

And then, to judge by a swath of furious, deep-cut inkless scratches on the paper, his ballpoint had gone totally dry.

Chapter Fifteen

He stood staring down at the table, bare of everything but the old, round-dial, faded black telephone and the message pad beside it, with those four scrawled words and those trenches of infuriated marks where the ballpoint had finally given out.

What did they mean those words in Conor's unmistakable writing, with all the emotion the scrawlingness of them showed? *Mum. Sorry I can't.*

Can't what? Can't find a pen that works? Only that? But no, even if Conor had lapsed into one of his childhood rages when his ballpoint stopped functioning, the wild energy with which the four words that had got on to the page had been written put that out of the question.

His eye fell on the ballpoint itself on the floor under the table, half-hidden by the pattern of the old threadbare carpet. He stooped, picked it up, mechanically tested it on a corner of the pad. Yes, totally out of ink.

In his mind's eye he saw Conor throwing it down. In some rage, of course. Anyone thwarted in that way might in a moment of exasperation have flung the wretched pen to the floor.

But the message itself, *Mum. Sorry I can't,* carried far more weight than that. Can't what? Can't stand any more of Superintendent Verney's hammer-hammer-hammer questioning? Well, yes. If Conor had never been told he was now no longer under suspicion, then the fear of yet another session with Verney, the ever-advancing tank, might well have started him writing such a message.

But then what had he done when the ballpoint ran out? How would that message have gone on? How? Would it . . . ?

Now, if ever, he thought, it's up to me to get into someone else's mind. To get into Conor's mind. My son. If I can only feel enough with him, with him as he sat here — No. No, as he stood here. That message was scrawled by someone standing up at this table, desperately stabbing down what was going through his mind.

He flipped up the page.

Yes, the force Conor had used had left a

discernible mark on the sheet below. He had never been sitting sensibly down to tell his mother he was going out to meet friends, or to give her some similar everyday message. No, he had been in a desperate state. When the ballpoint gave out he had plainly abandoned any attempt to write whatever it was he wanted to say.

And was the rest of that ferocious message going to be — the terrible idea had been there all along, to be fought away — *I can't go on any longer. I am going to end it all. Sorry, sorry, sorry?*

Something like that? And if so . . . Oh, God.

He whirled away from the table, strode to the door, flung open the kitchen door opposite, groped for the light, found it. As deserted as the sitting room on the other side. No fifteen-year-old boy lying on the floor with his head in the gas oven.

A door at the far end of the hall. Yanked open in its turn. The dark and fog. A bricked backyard and, only just to be made out, the garden beyond.

Almost hopeless to search there. Leave it for now.

Up the stairs. The pinched landing and four doors to choose from. First, bathroom. Empty, a wretched rust-stained tub, a basin

234

needing cleaning, towels draped over a couple of rails.

The door next to it. The loo. Tiny, and bare.

A touch of relief. Often the lavatory the place a suicide chooses. Past experience. But nothing here to hang oneself from.

The next door. Their bedroom. That bed she had boasted about — *And Mike was on top of me* — still unmade even this late in the day. Vicky had been a better housewife once. But never mind what this room said. What would the last door say, Conor's door?

His hand on the knob, he could not help standing there. Feeling, yes, his every limb fixed in stone.

But it was for a moment only. Then a twist of the knob, the door swept violently open.

And nothing.

No body hanging, dangling from some beam or hook. No Conor lying on the bed, face drained of all blood, whatever pills he had found having done their work.

He staggered into the room, and, scarcely realizing what he was doing, collapsed on to that same empty bed and sat, a slumped heap. Relief washing and washing through his mind.

But in a minute grim thoughts began to

scurry back and forth once more.

All right, Conor hasn't taken his life here in this house. But did he go somewhere else? Out into that dark garden? Is there anywhere there where he could have hanged himself? Some tree? God knows.

Or can it be he's just run away? From the prospect of further questioning? Or perhaps because he's been keeping the names of his friends from Verney? Belinda? Alec Gaffney? Someone else? Possibly, though it was unlikely, no more than relatively innocent buyers of a few Ecstasy tablets? And now had he suddenly doubted his ability to resist the pressure any longer?

But — But, if it is the worst, the very worst, and he has killed himself, who is to blame? In this very house, just two days ago, my wife, my almost ex-wife, Conor's own mother, told me she believed he had killed Professor Unwala because whenever he had done something wrong I had always seen why, always known how he felt, always found an excuse for him.

Apart from the fact that she probably never really thought Conor was a murderer, was she right? I persuaded myself soon enough afterwards that she was wrong. Or almost persuaded myself. I told myself I had been a good father. And I have been. I have.

But now . . . ? Now, if this is what Conor has done, if he has killed himself, how can I go on believing I brought him up well, made him a strong, confident personality? How do I now answer Vicky's charge?

Guilty.

Yes, now, looking back at all I did as a father, more, looking back on all I have ever done since I was a boy like Conor at Harrison, I must force myself to admit that I have all my life been too tolerant. That I have hugged to myself too often that one piece I remember from hated French. *Tout comprendre, c'est tout pardonner.*

Because it's wrong. All right, *comprendre*, understand everything, or as much as you possibly can. But don't then go on to pardon everything. Yes, whoever said that in France — whenever it was — did get it wrong. Though, in fact, didn't old Pasdore use to say it wasn't a proper quotation at all, that people had got hold of whatever it was originally and had softened it down?

So, admit to myself now I have often failed to do the hard thing. Not always, but frequently enough. And I failed because I so easily saw how and why someone — Conor, Vicky, a friend or acquaintance, a criminal I have had to deal with — had done whatever it was they had done, and I had pardoned them. Pardoned Conor when I should have checked him. Checked him hard when one of those rages of his swamped him. I should have shaken him, bellowed at him, brought him to his senses, told him that that was not the way to behave. Never the way to behave.

And would he have learnt the lesson? He might have done. The chances are, considering the way he seems naturally to behave decently, he would have accepted the rebuke. And even if he hadn't, I should still have tried to pull him up. Sharp and hard. I should have corrected him. Not just understood him.

So now — he rose heavy with weariness to his feet — the garden and what I may find there.

But is there a flashlight anywhere in this damn house? I'll need one. God knows, in the dark and with the fog still lying heavy — I can smell it, the sea tang, even in here — it will be hard enough to see anything. To find anything. But, flashlight or no flashlight, I've got to go and look.

To come upon his dangling body? Please God, no. Please God, no. But if he's there I must find him.

He tumbled down the stairs, jerked open the door of the sitting room. Flashlight.

Flashlight. Where would they keep it? At home it was always in the coat-stand drawer. They didn't have one here. No room. But would Vicky have put one in some similar place? Or Conor?

I could see Conor doing that in the same way as he carried on with the message-pad idea we had at home.

The message pad. Something I half-noticed about it. When — was it? — I flipped up the page to see the impression left by those ballpoint scratches. Something that meant something to . . .

He darted across to the table, lifted again the page on the spiral-topped pad.

And, yes.

Yes, this is what it was I saw. Saw without seeing. Under the wire spiral, this thin strip of torn paper. Someone had ripped out a sheet. The sheet after the one Conor began his message on.

Yes, almost for a cert he found something else to write with after all, and, yes, continued his message on a new sheet. Of course, those impressions from his scratch marks were in fact too faint, lighter than they should have been. The marks from the empty ballpoint had gone right through the sheet later torn out and on to the next one.

Torn out. But that must mean Vicky got

that message, the full message. And she pulled the sheet out of the pad, in her usual way.

And does that mean that whatever Conor wrote just told Vicky he was going to do something else, something less, than hang himself? And when she read that, had she gone off to look for him? It could be. Surely it must be.

Then, behind him, he heard the front door crash back as it was swung open. And became aware that, concentrating on the pad, he had been only subliminally conscious of a car coming to a fast stop just outside.

He turned.

Into the room came Vicky and, looming behind her sports-ace Mike, bursting out of a white high-neck pullover and blue blazer. Plainly unable to decide whether or not he should be subduing his everlasting grin.

'Phil,' Vicky shot out. 'What the hell are you doing here?'

He recovered himself.

'I came out to you because no one had answered the phone all afternoon and most of the evening, and when I arrived I found the front door open.'

Vicky swung round to her Mike.

'You mean to say you came out after me

and never even thought to lock the door?'

'But sweetheart, we were in such a hurry. Conor gone and everything.'

'Conor? Yes, where is he? What's happened to him? Do you know?'

'God knows where the damn boy is,' Vicky snapped.

'But — But his note on the pad? He left a message for you, didn't he? Did he say anything about — about killing himself?'

'Killing himself?' Vicky answered shrilly. 'Oh, come on. All he said was he was going away. Running away. Just wait till he comes back. I'll give him a message all right.'

'But the note here, the one he just began, it says *Mum. Sorry I can't.* And then his pen ran out.'

'Oh, Christ, I forgot. We've got what he really wrote with us. Show it to him, Mike, for Christ's sake.'

Mike felt first in one pocket of his brass-buttoned blazer and then in another and another. At last he brought out from a trouser pocket a roughly folded sheet. He handed it across.

Written with a soft, dark pencil, it said: *Mum. I'm sorry but I can't take any more from that boss of Dad's. The truth is I know what friends of mine thought of doing the night Prof Unwala was murdered. But I'm not going to betray them. They are my friends*

Then came two words that had been crossed through, *despite what.* And the message continued: *I know if I have to sit there being asked and asked I'll eventually give in. So I'm going. Somewhere well out of sight. Tell Dad.*

'Right,' he said. 'I think that makes it clear the silly fellow hasn't done anything disastrous. Thank God. So have you both been looking for him? I take it you've had no success?'

'Yes,' Vicky said, more quietly. 'I'd gone out to the shops just before lunchtime, and when I came back I found that note, and Conor gone. Plus whatever money I had in my dressing-table drawer.'

'And how much was that?'

'How the hell should — Oh, well, I suppose there must have been thirty or forty quid.'

'So, enough for Conor to have buzzed off to London. Or anywhere.'

'Yes. Yes, I don't know. When I phoned Mike we went to the station and the coach station as well as everywhere else we could think of. But nobody seemed to have seen a boy answering to Conor's description. Phil, what are we going to do?'

He felt a tiny glint of pleasure, of revengeful pleasure, in her appealing to him rather than to hulking, half-grinning Mike. But he quelled it.

'There are procedures,' he said. 'I'll see they're put in train. A Missing from Home notice. Circulating a description to all the neighbouring forces. Message to the Met. One of them may turn up trumps.'

Then he brought himself to face facts.

'But, on the other hand, it's only fair to say kids of Conor's age go missing by the hundred in the course of a year, and a good many of them stay missing for a long, long time.'

'And what he said in the note, that he'd only been so obstinate with your Mr Verney because he was shielding some friends, is that true? I mean, you don't think he did have something to do with the murder, do you?'

He almost groaned aloud.

'No. No, you see the bloody awful thing is Conor's been taken out of the frame. Altogether. It's been confirmed that at the time of the murder he was actually making his way back here.'

Now the familiar, furious speak-first, think-afterwards Vicky came swooping back.

'And you knew this all along? You knew that Conor was not going to be interrogated any more? You knew it. And you didn't care enough simply to ring me up and tell me. To tell him, even?'

He tried to stem the acid flow.

'No, look, I knew nothing about it. I was still off the case. It was Verney who should have told you and didn't. I suppose I can understand why. He'd a lot on his mind and —'

'Christ, Phil, will you for once in your life stop making excuses for people. A lot on his mind. For God's sake, what he ought to have had on his mind was that he'd been harassing and bullying a defenceless fifteen-year-old for hour after hour and when he found he'd got hold of the wrong person the least he could do was apologize. To fucking grovel, in fact.'

He was about to try to explain how Verney could reasonably have not informed her about Conor, when into his mind there flooded the resolution he had made sitting on Conor's bed not ten minutes earlier. He had confessed to himself there, believing Conor might very well have taken his own life, that he had been guilty over the years of being too tolerant. Especially in the way he had handled Conor. He had made some sort of a resolution, sitting on the bed there, to be harder in future. To *comprendre*, but not then unthinkingly to *pardonner.*

I made a resolution in fact not to be always *soft as a duck's arse.* So now let me tell Vicky she's right, however violently she's expressed herself. I shouldn't *pardonner* Verney.

'Yes, Verney was out of order. I admit that. However much he has on his plate with the media making all the fuss about Brilliant Nobel Scientist Slain, he damn well ought to have let you know. No getting away from that.'

'Well, I hope you bloody well tell him. To his face. I would. And I dare say one of these days I will.'

'I will, yes. If it comes up. But I must get back and start things going. Try not to worry too much. I reckon Conor'll think better of this in a day or two.'

'Yes, and what will you do then? Tell him he's been a good boy and Daddy understands?'

He gave her a rueful grin.

'Well, no. No, I don't think I will do that this time. And not for a long time to come, I hope.'

Chapter Sixteen

He got late to bed in his cold, empty house that night. But he was satisfied he had put in train every possible step towards finding Conor. Not that any sign of him had come to light.

He lay there on his side of the double bed, where as a baby Conor had romped with them both, and thought of where he might be. In London, likely as not. And without a bed. Lying in some squitty cardboard box in a doorway somewhere, if he had been lucky enough even to find a box. Or, perhaps worse, with a bed but in some house he had been lured to by a predatory pimp. Conor, for all his brightness, was still in many ways an innocent.

Exhausted with emotion as he was, it was not long before he fell asleep. But then he slept so heavily it was well past eight before some interior watchdog jerked him into consciousness, abruptly aware that he had to bring young Alec Gaffney in for questioning.

And Alec, he asked himself as, cancelling breakfast, he pulled on his clothes from the day before and hurried out, will he stand up to Verney as Conor managed to do? Just managed to do? Or will he crack inside half an hour?

He realized, as he came out and got into the car, that the fog had lifted. One good thing in this badly begun day.

But in the end how well had Conor stood up to Verney, always only just on the safe side of forbidden *oppressive questioning?* All right, Conor had succeeded in not naming the friend or friends he was protecting — Alec Gaffney? Belinda? Someone else? — but at what a cost. The mere prospect of another session with Verney sending him running desperately into hiding.

But where? Only as far away as Barminster, and happily sitting there over bacon and eggs in some cheap bed-and-breakfast place? It could be. It might only be that. And before the end of the day he could be back at the cottage and everything put right.

But be realistic, that was unlikely enough. The second message on the pad had shown more determination than that. *So I'm going. Somewhere well out of sight.*

Pulling up outside the estate agent Harold Gaffney's big house out on the far edge of the town, the sweep of lawn in front of it still sparkling with the moisture of last night's fog, he looked at his watch. Good. Time enough to get hold of Alec and get him down to the nick before nine, together with one parent or another as Appropriate Adult. And then?

Then will tank-crushing Verney in one brisk bout of hard questioning lay his hand on the murderer of Professor Unwala? Triumph before the ready-to-pounce media make life hell for the whole of Barshire Constabulary?

He rang the doorbell.

A maid, yellow duster half-concealed behind her back, answered. He made sure from her that Alec had not gone out and then asked for his father.

'Mr Gaffney's leaving for business any minute, sir.'

'Yes. I dare say. But I have to speak to him. Will you tell him it's Detective Chief Inspector Benholme, on a matter concerning his son.'

It did the trick. Harold Gaffney came out to him in the hall.

He realized then that he must have seen him at Harrison Academy functions over the years. A tall, lean man, taller even than his beanpole son, with what must once have been the same red hair now faded to a pale pepperiness echoed in a heavy moustache.

'What is this, Chief Inspector? I'm right, aren't I, in thinking my son and yours are at Harrison Academy together? In the same year?'

'They are. But can we go somewhere more private? I have something I have to tell you about your Alec.'

He saw a look of sharp surprise come into the washed-out blue eyes beneath the pale red bushy eyebrows, and thought he was going to be abruptly rebuffed.

But evidently Harold Gaffney had seen his own look of plain determination.

'Very well. But I trust what you have to say won't take long. I like to take a look in at our various offices on Saturday mornings and I'm usually gone by nine.'

He did not answer that, but followed the tall estate agent into a room that was evidently his study, two soft leather armchairs on either side of the fireplace in which a fire had been laid but not lit, a big partner's desk with a scatter of papers on it, dark almost patternless curtains, dim paintings of rural scenes.

'Well, Chief Inspector?'

He had not been invited to sit, and was glad of it.

'I have to tell you, sir, that I have come to take your son to King's Hampton police station to be questioned concerning his possible involvement in the murder of Professor Unwala in Sandymount last Monday.'

Harold Gaffney went a shade paler, but his blue eyes at once shot out an angry glare.

Well, I suppose I know how he feels, little though I like what I've seen of him. But what I felt when I first thought Conor might have killed the old man, that'll be what he's suddenly feeling now.

'Mr Benholme, can you really be meaning what you have said? I can't imagine Alec's ever been to Sandymount. An area like that. And I can assure you he's not the sort of boy to be involved in anything of that nature, not even peripherally.'

'I can well understand how you must feel, sir. But I can tell you Alec admitted to me when I had a word with him as he left school yesterday that he had indeed been in Sandymount. And at the time we know the murder took place.'

'Well, even if that's so, I still cannot see why you wish to take the lad down to the police station like a common criminal. Surely, if you've anything to ask him, you can do it here and now?'

'I am afraid not, sir. Detective Superintendent Verney is in charge of the inquiry, and he wishes to question your boy under proper conditions. And for that reason, too, we shall require him to be accompanied by an adult, preferably either yourself or his mother.'

'But, Chief Inspector, I've already told you I make the rounds of our offices on Saturday mornings, and, of course, it's out of the question for Mrs Gaffney to accompany Alec in circumstances like these. Surely you can make alternative arrangements?'

'I'm afraid that's impossible, sir. I would hesitate to suggest a gentleman of your standing was obstructing the police, but I must tell you that, if necessary, I would go along that route.'

Washed blue eyes fixed in a look of baleful fury.

'Well then, I suppose I shall have to comply. But — but I don't even know that Alec is still in the house.'

'He is, sir. So I was informed.'

A hot breath of thwarted rage.

'Very well, very well. Just let me call the boy and inform my wife. I suppose that won't be construed as obstructing you?'

'Not at all, sir.'

* * *

But, though it was barely three minutes past nine when he led Alec Gaffney, visibly trembling, face blotchily pale and red, into the interview room, there was a long, tense wait for Harold Gaffney's solicitor before Verney himself arrived. And then he found he was in for a surprise.

As he made to leave, duty done, Verney took hold of his elbow.

'No, Mr Benholme, I want you to assist at the interview, if you please.'

'Very good, sir.'

They sat down at the long green-surfaced table, Verney and himself on one side, with, opposite, Alec Gaffney, looking now almost at fainting point, his father gathered up for the fight, and Barham Williams, King's Hampton's top solicitor, known to all the CID as Baa-baa, doing the *gravitas* act.

Then Verney, before taking the twin tapes out of their plastic wrap, switching on the recording machine and explaining its function, leant towards him and whispered three words: 'Old routine, Phil.'

So that's his idea. The old routine, the one we used to do so often in the past. *Me hard: you soft.* If that's the way he wants it, no choice of course. But . . . But am I now the same softie who played that role so easily

252

in the old days? After what I learnt about myself when I thought I'd find Conor's body hanging from a tree in the garden there? No. No, I'm not. So how will I manage?

Well, I've play-acted being hard in the past when I thought some suspect would cough in the face of a show of toughness, and I brought it off. So I suppose I can play-act the softie now. I suppose I can . . .

At once Verney, daring Baa-baa Williams to utter the slightest objection, began going through the standard explanation for the recording. Time noted, those present named, two tapes being made, one for each party. On and on.

And then, with all the due precautions observed, it began.

'Right, lad, I want you to understand without any room for doubt what this is all about. It's about murder. It's about someone who battered to death a man called Edul Unwala in a house in Percival Road, Sandymount, on Monday last. Now, do you understand that?'

Verney's words thump-thump-thumping out like blows from a steam hammer.

Alec Gaffney swallowed hard, tried to speak, failed. Beside him Baa-baa Williams leant forward.

But at last Alec managed to choke out a word.

'Yes.'

'Yes? You understand I am inquiring into a murder?'

'Yes. Yes, I do.'

Alec's hand, clutching the edge of the table, was already leaving sweaty smears on the polished green surface.

'Right. Now, as I said, Edul Unwala was murdered in his house in Percival Road, Sandymount, at — we know this almost to the minute, remember — six P.M. on Monday last. Now, where were you at that time, lad?'

He's headed right into it, old Verney. The crunch straight away. Christ, I feel sorry for the kid, guilty or not.

Twice Alec tried to answer. Only at the third attempt did he succeed.

'I — I don't know where I was. Not exactly. That's almost a week ago. I can't remember.'

'But you were seen, lad. You were seen in Percival Road itself.'

Baa-baa jumped in.

'You don't have to answer, Alec. If you cannot recall where you were, you can't.'

'All right, young Alec, don't answer.

Don't say a word. As Mr Williams has been so quick to tell you, that's your right. But I have my rights too, you know. And one of them is the right to draw conclusions.'

The look across the shiny green surface of the table was as unyielding as steel.

'But — but — listen, well, it is true I was —'

Baa-baa pounced again.

'Alec, remember —'

'No, no. It's no use. I was down there. Mr Benholme told me yesterday I'd been seen. Oh, what's the bloody use. I was there. Yes.'

Verney had not taken his eyes once from Alec's face, shiny with perspiration all over now.

'Yes, you were there. In Sandymount. And now tell me what you did there. And, remember, it's no use inventing and lying and trying to get out of it. We know you were in Sandymount. We know Professor Unwala was murdered in Sandymount, and we know when. So, now, let's hear just what happened.'

'No. No. Nothing happened. All right, all right, I was down that way on Monday. I was in the shop at the corner of Percival Road. But that was all. You can ask —'

A silence.

'Yes, lad? Who can we ask?'

'You can . . .'

A longer pause. Tongue flicking out to wet lips, like a lizard's.

'Who can we ask, lad?'

'Yes. Yes, that's it. You can ask the people in that shop. They'll remember us. Me. They'll remember me. Me. I — I tried to buy — Well, all right, I tried to buy some whisky, and they wouldn't bloody well let me have any.'

Harold Gaffney swung round to his son.

'What the hell were you doing buying whisky? You know the very taste of it makes you physically sick. We've had more than one disgusting exhibition of that. And what were you doing in Sandymount in any case? A son of mine . . .'

'Mr Gaffney.' Verney's voice iron-hard. 'I am here to ask your son certain questions. If you attempt to ask him questions of your own, I shall have no alternative but to suspend this interview and detain your son in custody until I have your assurance you will not interfere.'

'Very well, very well. But . . . Well, to hear that the boy's been in the habit of frequenting that malodorous part of the town . . . All I can say is he'll have words from me when this is over.'

Now. Time for my soft intervention.

'But you are in the habit of going down to Sandymount, Alec,' he said. 'That's true, isn't it?'

Alec gave his father a quick glance, mingling fear and boyish anger. And then he turned with a look of pure insolence.

'I'm sure that's one of the things Mr Williams would tell me I needn't answer.'

Well, I do seem to have lost my soft-man touch.

Verney, flashing him a quick look of disapproval, leant an inch further towards his victim.

'And I've already told you, lad, what conclusions I draw from clever-dick answers like that. Now, let's hear the truth. You go down to Sandymount often enough, don't you? And why do you go there, lad? Eh? Why?'

'None of your —'

Baa-baa leaping in to save his client from the wrath evidently about to burst on him.

'Mr Verney, I am within my rights, my rights, to advise Alec here when he should or should not answer questions.'

'Oh, yes? And I suppose you'll advise him to answer nothing. Your rights. His rights. And I tell you both again, I've got my rights. To think whatever I choose to in the face of tactics of that sort. Now, lad, let's hear it. Why do you go down to Sandymount?'

'It's — it's — Oh, hell, you might as well know. We're not the only ones. I — I mean, I'm not the only one. I'm not. The bloody police must know what goes on in the town, I suppose. You must know how many Saturday-night raves there are. And what you take before you go.'

'Ecstasy,' Verney snapped in. 'Oh, yes, lad. We know all about Ecstasy. Where you can get it, how you can get it. So that's what you've been doing, is it?'

And is that, after all, all the stupid boy's been doing? Is this what all that evasion's been about? That he was down there, as I did think at one stage, to buy Ecstasy and for no other reason? Have we got it all wrong about the murder? Was this all Conor was trying to shield his mate from?

But Verney had not finished.

'All right, lad. You were breaking the law. Ecstasy's a prohibited substance. But —' A tiger smile. 'But we won't bother with that. Not at all. Just so long as you tell us who you were with down there. Who's this "we", we've been hearing mentioned and then rowed back from? You tell me that.'

Well done him. I'd noted the hesitations and withdrawals, but I hadn't thought of pursuing them. Not keeping up enough pressure? Could be. And I ought to be pressuring him hard, when I'm sitting here. Even if I never say a word. It's what's needed. The looming figure, silently asking. Demanding.

But in any case, I think I know the answer Verney'll get. I'm sure I do, in fact. It's Belinda. Belinda Withrington's been going down to Sandymount with Alec to buy Ecstasy. No doubt about it. But Conor? Was he one of the party? Well, I'd take a bet he wasn't, or not to go buying Ecstasy. But perhaps I'm about to be proved wrong. What if instead of saying *Belinda Withrington* Alec now bursts out with *Conor Benholme?*

'Mr Williams, do I have to answer that?'

Baa-baa all smiley reassurance.

'No, not at all, Alec. As I've already explained you don't have to —'

'Oh, damn it all. Mr Benholme here knows anyhow. His sneaking son, Conor, will have told him. So there's no point in keeping it secret. OK, it was Belinda Withrington I was there with on Monday. We often go down there. And, yes, make of it what you like, I don't care, it's to get hold of a few E's at the weekends.'

Verney did not bother to look pleased. He gave Alec another of his stony, tank-driver looks.

'But what about the whisky, lad? Why did you and this Belinda girl want whisky on Monday evening? Why was that, I wonder?'

It was plain that this seemingly inconsequential question had hit a dangerous area. Alec's face went tense as if it were corded inside.

'Now, Alec, I want to know. Why exactly were you trying to buy yourself whisky at that shop at the end of Percival Road last Monday?'

No answer.

'I asked you why, lad.'

Still no answer. Now Alec was looking down at an imaginary spot of the clear green surface of the table in front of him as if he was determined never to look anywhere else.

'I'm going to hear your answer, lad. Make no mistake about that. If we sit here till ten o'clock tonight I'm going to hear.'

'Mr Verney,' Baa-baa Williams sounded deeply, deeply shocked. 'Mr Verney, my client, as you well know, is entitled to refreshment from time to time, and to periods of relief. There can be no question of his still being here at ten o'clock this evening.'

'No, Mr Williams, I'm sure there can't be. Because your client is going to answer my question. Now.'

And Alec did answer.

'I was trying to buy some whisky to get my courage up. And that's the whole truth.'

But I bet he's only come up with that because that cunning old devil Baa-baa has given him a breathing space. The boy's pleased with himself now, however much he's trying to conceal it. So what'll Verney do now?

'All right. So you wanted to get your courage up. Just what for, lad?'

The question cracked whip-like.

Look at Alec's face now. It'd be a comical sight in any other circumstances. But not now. It's plain to me. By inventing that answer he overstepped the mark and he's just realized it. He wouldn't be the first to make a mistake like that under Verney's pressure.

'I — I — I just wanted to get my courage up to — Yes, to buy some E.'

Verney was implacable.

'Oh, yes? That's what it was, was it? So how does it come about that one moment you're telling me you go down to Sandymount regularly to get your little supplies, and the next you're saying you can't get the courage up to buy any without downing a bottle of whisky?'

Downing a bottle of whisky. Or a half-bottle as Mrs Damberry told me, and I told

Verney, briefing him.

But, hey, Alec can't take whisky. Didn't his dad say so not ten minutes ago?

He leant forward beside Verney.

'Alec, that can't be right, you wanting whisky. It makes you sick, doesn't it?'

The soft question, softly put.

And this time it worked.

'Oh God, it was — It was for Belinda, if you must know. She wanted it. But she doesn't look as old as I do, and so she told me to say I was eighteen and insist on getting it. But . . . But they wouldn't let me have it anyhow.'

'Trying to hide behind a girl now, are we?'

Hard Verney came bouncing in.

Oh, God, the fool. I'd got it out of him, and now he's banging in saying he doesn't believe him. We were beginning to get somewhere, I swear it. But now . . .

'Oh, damn it, think what you like. I don't care. You're just trying to trap me into saying I did something I never did do. Well, go on then, go on. But I won't give you the satisfaction of hearing another word from me.'

'Mr Verney,' Baa-baa put in now, at his smoothest. 'May I suggest my client has been tried too far?'

Verney's mouth shut in a grim line.

I do believe he's seen where he's gone wrong. The hard man.

And, hard or not, Verney clearly knows when he's been beaten.

'Very well, Mr Williams, I think perhaps we'll take a break now. We'll resume, shall we say, after lunch. Two o'clock suit you?'

Chapter Seventeen

Verney, as soon as the Gaffneys and Baa-baa Williams had gone, took him into his own office. Big desk, clear but for brass pen tray, empty in-basket, empty out-basket, one red telephone, one black. Looming bookcase filled with bound copies of the *Police Gazette*. Above them a row of gleamingly polished golf trophies.

Shutting the door, Verney turned to him.

'I told you we were to play it the old way. You only opened your mouth on a couple of occasions, and then you made a muck of it. What's got into you?'

What's got into me? How can I say to him that only last night I thought my son had committed suicide because I had been too tolerant, and that I resolved I'd keep that weakness of mine in check for ever more? I can't say that. So what do I say?

'I did my best, sir.'

'And a pretty poor best it was. I suppose

you were sitting there feeling sorry for that little tyke. So, when we have our next go at him, what line would you, in your wisdom, care to take?'

He thought rapidly.

Let the sarcasm slide over him? Say *I leave that to you, sir?* But if that little tyke in fact took that cricket bat to old Professor Unwala, then he's got to be made to admit it. So, tell Verney what I can't help feeling would do that? Yes or no?

Yes.

'I don't like to say this, sir, but it's my impression the boy's actually too scared of you to let himself come out with anything at all. Whether all he's doing is trying to keep that girl, Belinda Withrington, out of trouble, or whether he did kill the old man, either way I've got the feeling he's too dead frightened to say anything.'

'Too frightened? A nasty little squit like that can't be made to be too frightened, Mr Benholme. Putting the fear of God in them's the way to get a cough. As you should know by now.'

A glare.

Then he marched round to the far side of his desk and sat himself in his tall leather chair.

'Now I'll tell you what we're going to do,'

he went on, tilting back as far as the chair would go. 'You were right about one thing at least. What we've got to establish is that the boy was in that room where the murder took place. All right, we've no evidence. There wasn't anything the Fingerprint officer could read, was there? Bookcase well wiped, bolts on the french windows hardly touched. And otherwise a jumble of dabs dating back to God knows when. Yes?'

'Yes, sir.'

'Right then, we'll take a little liberty and put it to the boy we've found some dabs that may've been left by the killer. That alone, that word *may*, could crack him. And, if it doesn't, we'll bloody well go on to take his prints, making as much of a business of it as we can. If he goes on holding out on us after that, I'll keep a close eye on old Baa-baa, but I'll say something to make the little tick believe we've got a match. Then we'll see.'

Tough tactics. And will they do it? Still, I suppose he could be right. Sometimes tough tactics the only way. That poor long streak of piss, Alec, though. All the same if he is the long streak of piss who hefted up that cricket bat . . . And I think he is. I think he must be. So . . .

'Yes, sir. That's clever. I reckon it may

266

very well do the trick. Almost for a cert, in fact.'

Verney's big, red-flushed face showed faint signs of gratification.

'And what about that runaway lad of yours, Phil?' he said, with a sudden change of direction. 'Any news?'

'Haven't heard anything, sir.'

'Well, cooped up with me in the interview room you hardly could. You'd better hop off now and see if anything's come in. I'll want you again this afternoon, but let's hope by then you've heard something. Ninety cases out of a hundred you do.'

'Yes, sir. Thank you.'

So, under that hard front some thought for others? Pretty well the first time I've ever seen it. But nice to find it's there. If only once in a long while.

There was no news of Conor. Nothing had come in as a result of his messages of the night before. Vicky, when he brought himself to phone her, had heard nothing. He even made a dash for his own deserted house, in the faint hope that Conor might have chosen to go back there. But no Conor, no message on the answerphone, nothing.

He tried to tell himself that no news was good news, and succeeded to the extent of feeling no news was not bad news. And then he forced himself to forget he was the father of a runaway son and remember he was a detective officer of the Barshire police investigating the murder of Edul Unwala, former Nobel Prize winner, aged researcher perhaps on the point of finding an answer to the miseries of Alzheimer's.

So who, he asked himself back in his own office with a hastily snatched sandwich, did kill the old man? If it was really Alec Gaffney, why? Why had he gone to that house and killed an old, defenceless man? The notion of the Hampton Hoard and Alec trying to get money to buy Ecstasy by finding it was looking more and more unlikely. The boy, apparently, had had no difficulty up to now in getting together enough cash for regular visits to Sandymount. So why at this point should he have urgently needed a lot more? All right, he might have upgraded to something costing a good deal more, but there had been no sign this morning of him having been on anything.

So is Verney wrong? Can't see myself suggesting that to him, though. Or not yet. Not at least till he's worked his fingerprints trick.

But if that doesn't come off? If at the end of the afternoon it's really clear Alec's innocent, as innocent as Conor, then who is in the frame? No one. No one with half the case against them as we've got against Alec. And, damn it, that's not all that good.

So, who?

He looked at his watch.

Ten to two. Better get down there. Verney may have had other thoughts, some other make-or-break tactic. And want me to play the softie? Or the hard man?

And the softie I can certainly do without. Being made to think all over again of my mistake with Conor. Conor, gone, lost, down in London, in danger, hungry, without hope.

'Mr Verney,' Baa-baa Williams leant forward, with his air of never doing any harm to anyone, 'before that recording instrument is switched on, may I simply say this? I was very much aware this morning that you were pressing this young lad to the utmost bounds of what is permissible. I trust that, when we are being recorded now, you will not go as far as you did before.'

Stony-faced reception.

'Mr Williams, I shall do as I think fit. I shall do my duty as I see it.'

'Very well, perhaps you should activate the recorder. I am beginning to think it's a pity I didn't make such remarks as I felt necessary while they were going on record. For a court perhaps to hear.'

Verney, by way of answer, simply leant across and pressed the switch on the machine.

They went through the formal ritual once again. Time, date, persons present, statutory warning recalled.

'Right, now, Alec. When we finished this morning you were telling me I was trying to trap you into admitting things you had never done. So just what was it you claim you didn't do?'

No answer.

So, as I'm in the softie shoes, chance here to jump in without committing myself more deeply than I want?

'For the tape. Alec Gaffney, though a little distressed, appears to have taken in what Detective Superintendent Verney asked him, and he has made no reply.'

Trust Verney likes that.

A half-glance of approval, I think. Let's see where he goes from here.

'All right then, lad, let me put it to you quite straight. Did you kill Mr Edul Unwala?'

Clear enough who's playing the hard man. If playing's the word. He's not capable of doing anything much else. But what reaction's he getting? Alec gone bloody white, that's for sure.

Christ, this going to be it? So soon? So quickly? The cough?

But at last Alec managed to voice an answer.

'No. No, no, no. I never killed him. I never touched him. Why should I? What'd he ever done to me? I didn't even see —'

But apparently he thought he had said enough.

Verney leant across the green-topped table till his heavy-set face was as near as he could get it to Alec's.

'And suppose,' he said, 'I was to tell you that fingerprint experts have been over and over that room where the old man was killed, and that they have a fine selection of unknown prints on file?'

It looked as if the shot had gone right home. Alec twisted his head from side to side, to Baa-baa Williams, to his father. A hunted animal.

Under the table Verney's knee gave him an urgent nudge.

He braced himself.

'Look, Alec, if you've got anything to tell us, now is the time, eh? Don't make it any harder for yourself. We're on your side, you know, when it comes down to it. We just want to get at the truth.'

He looked unwaveringly at the boy, trying to glow with compassion.

But am I really feeling it? Conveying it? And how is he reacting to me? Jesus, I wish that face of his was some sort of VDU screen, flashing up the thoughts inside. Damn it, I can see some emotion, some bloody strong one, is occupying his whole mind. But I'm buggered, try as I may, if I can get inside that skull of his.

So much for gift of understanding.

So I've lost it? Now that I'm striving to be less bloody tolerant, have I lost that prized ability of mine?

God knows.

At last Alec exploded into speech, an indignant screeching denial.

'I don't believe it. I don't believe it. I don't believe you've got any stinking finger-prints.'

So, no go. Fighting on.

And what does that outburst mean? Guilty? Guilty, and reduced to hoping against hope? Or is he somehow in the clear? But if he is, he's still got something to hide. He must have. Why else did he flame up like that? But what? What's he hiding? Wish I had even a glimmering.

'Very well, lad,' Verney said, making his

voice ominously smooth. 'Shall we take your fingerprints? See what we find?'

Glower.

'Do what the hell you like.'

Verney turned to Harold Gaffney, moulding his face into a semblance of a smile.

'Mr Gaffney, do you give your consent, as the Appropriate Adult at this interview, to your son's fingerprints being taken?'

'Alec?' his father asked.

'I already said: I don't care.'

And Verney, of course, ordered him to supervise the fingerprint taking.

He's right, though. Should be me doing it. Keeping the bloody pressure up. God knows, if it's left just to some WPC she may smile at him, crack some joke. And bang, he'll get back all his cockiness. But with suddenly-transformed-into-hard-man Detective Chief Inspector Benholme there, grim-faced, it'll be a very different matter.

'Very good, Alec,' he said. 'Shall we go? Mr Gaffney, do you wish to be present?'

'I'm not a bloody ten-year-old,' Alec snapped.

Good sign. He's really feeling the pressure now. Whether it's just Verney's questioning or whether it's knowing he put prints there when he yelled out *You black bastard,* he's good and worried. That's for sure.

But that yell? It was high-pitched, Mrs Ahmed certain about that. And Alec's voice is well broken. So, are we all — No. No, by God. When Alec reacted to Verney's tough little tactic with the *fingerprint experts* — experts, whole imaginary team of them, the cunning old bugger — then his voice wasn't so adult. No, that *I don't believe it. I don't believe it.* Under that much strain his voice had been a real screech.

Which means it could be him, and he could well be on the point of cracking. Just as I'm taking his prints? Because I think I've got to do that myself. If I can remember the exact procedure. But my hand pressing his fingers down, that'll add one more degree to the pressure he's under. One more nerve-breaking degree.

Poor kid.

Murdering kid?

He led the boy — victim or killer — off in the direction of the Fingerprint Room. Outside the little washroom next door to it he paused.

'I suppose this is as good a time as any,' he said, 'to tell you that, if your fingerprints are not required as evidence, they will be destroyed. You have the right to witness that being done. So in the event that your prints are not needed' — he put a strong, lingering emphasis on the *not,* one more jab of pressure — 'would you wish to exercise that right?'

'Yes. No. Oh, I don't know. What's it matter?'

'Well, I shall record you as wishing to witness their destruction, if it should arise. Now, come into this room here with me and I want you to wash your hands. Wash them well. And then dry them very thoroughly.'

I'm making a meal of all this, but every police-officer order I give him screws up the heat one notch more.

He watched while Alec sluiced his hands, reddened with the interior pulsing of blood, under the cold tap and then, on the thin, damp roller towel hanging beside the sink, began to dry them.

'Better than that, please. Do it again, and then get them completely dry. We need perfect impressions.'

At last he marched him into the Fingerprint Room itself.

A WPC, one whose name he did not know, was there, as he had thought there might be.

'I'm going to take this young gentleman's prints,' he said to her, voice in the official mode. 'Please ink up for me.'

They watched in silence while she squeezed oily black ink out of a monster tube and then with the well-grimed wooden roller spread it carefully over the heavy copper plate on the counter.

'Right,' he said when the process was over, 'let me fill in the particulars on the Fingerprints form in the frame over here and then we'll be ready.'

He took his time, peering down at the heavy-paper form clamped in its metal frame at the other end of the counter. By his side he could feel the heat emanating from Alec's gangly body.

Good. Good. Stew, lad. Stew.

'Now,' he said at last, 'give me your right hand.'

Alec thrust it out. Despite the cold water poured over it not five minutes earlier it was already beginning to glisten with sweat. He took a tight grip of the forefinger, placed it firmly down on the inky surface of the plate, moved with Alec over to the clamped form, keeping an unrelenting grip all the while, and subjected the pad of the finger to the correct rolling motion, which, just in time, he remembered from his earlier days.

'All right, middle finger now.'

Back to the ink stone, keeping a blank,

uncommunicative silence. Then over again to the form.

'Good. Ring finger next.'

As he transferred his grasp he could distinctly feel that this finger was sweatier than the forefinger had been, probably even sweatier than the middle finger.

Won't give a very clear impression. But as this is all nothing more than jiggery-pokery, doesn't matter. Unless that WPC notices and tries to put me right.

The rolling motion in the appropriate square on the absorbent paper of the form.

Now shift myself round a bit — wish I could remember the lass's name — make sure she can't see too well. Little frown on her face. Better be careful. Don't want the whole show spoiled.

'Very good. Now your little finger.'

Ink it well. Press really hard, even harder than I really should. Not a flicker on my face. Over to the form. Roll the finger. Good.

'Thumb now.'

At last, leading him back to the ink slab to begin on his left hand, he felt the pulse in the wrist he had just changed his hold to begin to throb violently.

Is this it? Is he going to crack now?

He took the forefinger, moved with deliberate slowness over the glistening black surface of the copper plate, brought the finger down slowly at last, inked it with care.

But, leading the boy for the sixth time to the form stretched in its metal frame, he realized that the throbbing in his wrist, instead of growing faster, was suddenly less intense.

What's gone wrong? I thought I'd got him. What the hell's gone wrong?

Then he saw. Across on the other side of the counter the WPC had a faint lingering smile on her face.

Christ, she's done something to reassure him. Winked? Shrugged? Something, anything. And whatever it was, it's saved him. Guilty or not guilty, guilty of murder or guilty of some lesser offence, he feels he's not alone any more. He feels able to cope.

What to do? Well, one thing. If that girl, whatever her name is, ever tries to get into CID, she's rejected. But what about young Alec here?

There was only one course left. He knew it. Carry on with the charade. Never do to let the boy see it's all been a hoax. If he tells old Baa-baa, we could find ourselves talking to the Police Complaints Authority.

No, it's all down to Verney now. If there's anything to be rescued from the cock-up.

Back into the interview room. Verney sitting where he had been, ready to rumble forward into battle. Opposite, Harold Gaffney and Baa-baa evidently trying to hold some sort of a neutral conversation. As he ushered Alec in he caught the words '. . . can never tell with house prices'. Then they broke off, as if they had been discovered exchanging dirty stories.

Just behind Alec's back he gave Verney a minute shake of the head. No joy.

Difficult to interpret that quick look back. Fury? Acceptance of the inevitable? Never mind, I've done my best. Hard man never allowed himself to relax for an instant. Not till that silly bitch spoilt it all. And that was hardly her fault, really. I should have warned her what I was up to. Only how could I have done? Having to keep Alec on a tight rein the whole time like that.

Ah, well. See if Verney can pull something out of the hat.

'Right, I'll just put the regulation words on to the tape again, and then I shall want to ask you once more what I've been asking before.'

Ritual completed, Verney leant heavily across.

'Now, while we're waiting to know what

279

our fingerprint people over at Headquarters in Barminster make of the impressions they've just had faxed to them . . .'

He allowed his voice to trail away.

Well, will he be able to stoke up the pressure again? That line about faxing the prints to HQ impressive enough. But is the boy, in fact, our intolerant killer? Or is he just a stupid youngster who's got himself, and Conor's Belinda, Conor's ex-Belinda, into trouble?

Whichever, plainly Alec has now regained enough confidence to look squarely back at Verney.

'All right, let's go over again what you've told us so far. You've admitted you were down in Sandymount at six o'clock on Monday evening last, the time Mr Edul Unwala was murdered. You —'

'No. No, it's true I was in Sandymount. In that shop. But that was at round about five. You've just said the murder didn't happen till six, and we weren't — I wasn't in Sandymount at all then.'

Verney was unfazed.

'Where were you then, lad? It's not enough, you know, to swear black and blue you weren't somewhere, you've got to tell us where you were. And it'd be a lot better for you if you could provide some reliable witnesses. Because, remember, we've got a witness, a reliable witness, who saw someone, someone in a black jacket like the Harrison Academy uniform, lurking at the other end of Percival Road for a good twenty minutes just before six o'clock.'

Good old Verney stretching a point again. I don't know how *reliable* old asthmatic Mr Jones would look if we ever had to put him in the witness box, and, as far as I remember, he was none too sure he'd seen that figure in the fog for as long as twenty minutes. Nor did he call it *lurking*. However . . . If it all gets Alec's attempt to give himself an alibi to fall down who's going to object? Not even old Baa-baa.

'I bet he didn't see me — I bet he didn't see whoever was there well enough to identify them. Or you'd have had an identity parade, wouldn't you?'

But Verney was not going to take insolence of that sort.

'I've half a mind to play back the tape to you, lad. Just to let you hear exactly what you said only half a minute ago. "I bet he didn't see me." Those were your exact words. *Me. Me. Me.* That's what you said. He didn't see you well enough to identify you, that's what you were boasting about. And what I say to you now is: there's no need to identify you. You've just told me out of your own mouth that you were standing there at the end of Percival Road shortly before Mr Unwala was beaten to death at number twelve.'

And it was enough. Alec's head dropped as though he had been pole-axed.

'Yes.'

The word was almost inaudible.

But Verney, instead of pouncing on it, demanding it be repeated, left a silence. Which, after some long seconds, Alec filled of his own accord.

'It's no use,' he said, speaking with strangulated clarity. 'I was there. Whoever you said saw me did see me. I was there at the end of Percival Road.'

'And then,' Verney came quietly in, 'you walked up to that house, you conned the old man into letting you in and then you battered him to death. Yes? Yes? Wasn't that the way it was?'

'No.'

A *No* uttered with perfect calm. A simply stated truth.

Chapter Eighteen

They had all been rocked. The *No* had been said with such plain firmness it was all but impossible not to believe it was the truth. No, Alec had stated, no, I did not go into number twelve Percival Road, for all that I admit I was standing in the road outside. Even Verney, who had been almost plunging across the table to deliver his final question, had seemed totally taken aback. He had swung away till his chair had creaked almost to breaking point. Harold Gaffney had switched in an instant from giving his son, the murderer, a look of incredulous disgust to a blank lack of comprehension. Baa-baa Williams had slowly removed the veiny hands which he had held in front of his face as Verney had battered out his accusation.

He himself had wondered for a moment if he had actually heard the *No*, clearly and firmly spoken though it had been.

But I did hear it. And young Alec, then,

did not do it. I can't believe anything else now. The pressure we've put him under, and at last that single, clear, decisive *No*.

God knows why he's resisted up till now. There must be more to it. Though I've no idea what it is. But he's innocent. At least of murder. Whatever else he may have done, he did not kill Edul Unwala. I know that now. We all know it. Even Verney.

But it was Verney who recovered first.

'All right,' he said, slowly bringing himself forward again, 'so you did not kill Mr Unwala. Very well, lad, if you say so. But don't tell me you don't know something about that death. Don't tell me you haven't been straining and struggling to keep something from us all this while. And now you're going to tell us about it. Right?'

'I've got nothing more to say.'

Alec pushed himself round to face Baabaa Williams.

'Mr Williams, I don't have to answer their questions, do I?'

'No, no, my boy. You're perfectly within your rights to answer "No comment" if you wish. Yes. And I think I'd advise you to do just that.'

'But I would not.'

Verney was back in action once more. Tank gun spitting harsh fire.

'Listen to me, Alec Gaffney,' he growled out. 'I am investigating a case of murder. A particularly brutal and vicious murder. And it is the duty of everyone who may know anything which could lead to the arrest of the perpetrator of that murder to assist the police in whatever way they can. Now, it's plain to me, and equally plain to Detective Chief Inspector Benholme here, that you know something that will lead directly to the apprehension of that murderer. So, I am asking you: what is it you have been keeping from us?'

'I — I can't say.'

'Won't say.'

'All right, won't say, if that's how you want it. But I won't. I won't. And that's that.'

Verney leant an inch nearer, and dropped his voice to the point where it seemed he was talking to Alec and Alec alone.

'Now, you've told us you did not kill Edul Unwala. And I'm inclined, I tell you frankly, to believe you. But what I am not inclined in any way to believe is that you know nothing about his murder. I am inclined to believe in fact that you saw it done.'

'No.'

But this *No* was distinctly different from that earlier firm and clear denial. There was in it, not to be mistaken, a note of hysteria.

Verney was quick to follow up.

'No? You deny you were in that house when the poor old man was battered down? Well, I wonder whether in just a minute or two I won't be in possession of evidence that tells me the exact contrary.'

He swung round to address the recording machine more directly.

'Detective Chief Inspector Benholme is now leaving the room in order to collect a fax message from Fingerprints Section at Barshire Police Headquarters.'

Going it a bit, aren't you? Wonder what all the lawyers will make of that when they listen to the tapes. *In order to collect a fax message from Fingerprints Section.* As if it would be ready in anything like this time. However . . . Detective Chief Inspector Benholme knows how to play his part when he gets the tip.

He got up, even making a performance of slapping his hands down on the table for the benefit of the machine. Let alone of Alec Gaffney.

Outside, he looked at his watch.

Give it five minutes? No, probably a bit less. Don't want this new pressure Verney's built up to fizzle away. But can he bring it off? Or are we going to end up as much in the dark as when it was clear Conor was off the hook?

Conor.

My Conor. Where are you? Will I ever see you again? Will we ever get back to our old life? Or . . . Or to today's version of it, you there with your mum and that bloody Mike, me seeing you at home every now and again. Unless I do sell the place, move into a flat. But oh, for the real old life. Sitting round the kitchen table for meals, talking about your prospects, how well you'll do in your A levels . . . God, he may never take them now. Never. A drifter in London, drugs, a rent boy, Aids. All that, instead of treasure-hunting holi— No, detectorist. Detectorist. And the chance of getting in to Cambridge, getting a degree in archaeology —

He forced himself to stop. Before his racing mind pictured yet worse calamities.

Before I bloody break down and weep.

Come on, think. Think what you're here for, Phil Benholme. Detective Chief Inspector Benholme. To assist in Detective Superintendent Verney's cunning ploy.

Right. So what have I got to do? Go back to the interview room — *Detective Chief Inspector Benholme has just re-entered* — and make Alec Gaffney believe I've just heard

287

from HQ that they've found some dabs that correspond —

Oh my God. A fax. I've got to go in there carrying a fax, pull the trick off properly. To find out, perhaps, if Verney's guess is right and Alec was at least in the house, was watching when someone — Who? Who? — killed the old man.

'Detective Chief Inspector Benholme has re-entered the room, bringing a fax message.'

Jesus, Verney's going it. Trust he'll keep a straight face when he sees the Daily Crime Bulletin sheet I snatched off Bob Carter's desk. Best I could find in the circs.

Oh, but yes. Should have known I could rely on Verney. Look at the way he's perusing that sheet. Perusing: the word. And now . . . Leaning forward again. Into battle.

'Yes. As I thought, two distinct prints, not whole but cleanly lifted. Of course, not proof . . .'

Verney leant back in his chair.

'Do you know anything about the law and fingerprints, Alec?'

Abruptly playing the soft man. Or his inept version of it. An over-rich avuncular act. Pathetic, really. But may work.

'No? Well, I'll explain a bit. Under the law of this country fingerprints identification is held not to be valid unless sixteen points, as we call them, sixteen places in the print of a suspect's finger, whichever finger it may be . . .'

He's building it up and up. Hope his little card castle won't tumble down.

'. . . are found precisely to correspond. Fifteen points only, on some incomplete fingermark lifted at the scene of a crime and our Fingerprint officer does not even go into the witness box, although those of us investigating the crime know perfectly well that fifteen points indicate just as surely as sixteen that our suspect was at the scene. As do fourteen points, thirteen, twelve, or even most probably ten. But the courts don't recognize that. They would hold that putting up an FPO to give evidence would constitute an attempt to influence a jury. You follow me so far?'

'I don't see what all this is in aid of.'

And sweat there on the boy's forehead? Certainly looks like it. A sheen. So Verney's getting somewhere.

'You don't see? Well, it's just that I'm trying to make sure you understand exactly the implications of the message I have in my hand here. You see, it tells me that your prints do not bear sixteen identical points to those we found.'

Palpable relief.

Verney, situation beautifully set up, sprang his trap.

'What there is mention of, however, is twelve points. Twelve points on one of the prints, and eleven on another.'

It worked.

Alec's face, till that moment simply expressing moderate confidence, looked abruptly shattered.

'So tell us . . .' Verney said softly.

'All right, it's true I was in there. But — but — But not on Monday. It was — It was the Friday before. Truly. It was. You must believe me. It — it was all so damn silly.'

'Go on.'

Alec gave a tremendous swallow.

'We — I was down in Sandymount to — Well, to buy some E for the weekend. And — and I just happened to be walking along Percival Road on my way there when the door of that old house — of number twelve opened. And this little old Indian called out to me. "My mouse," he said. "It's my mouse. Catch it. Catch it." Well, he was looking at the path to his gate, and when I looked there was a little white mouse crouching there on the red and black tiles. So, well, I didn't much want to, but I opened the gate and made a dive for it. And I caught it. Then the old chap told me to bring it in, and I went in with him and there were all those cages with other mice in them. One of them had its door slightly ajar, and the old man asked me to put the mouse in there. And I — well, first of all it escaped again. But I managed to catch it all right, and I got it into the cage, but I knocked the old boy's specs down behind . . .'

The oddly convincing story abruptly trailed away.

As much to round it off as anything he put a softman's question.

'You knocked his spectacles down, and then what? Did you pick them up for him? Or what?'

He got no immediate answer.

'Well, go on. I mean, you did find them, the specs, I suppose. But then what? Was Professor Unwala grateful? Did he — what? — offer you a drink before you left? Well, no, not a drink. But tea? Or some money? Or what?'

Alec continued to look almost as uneasy as when he had been trying to lie his way out of having been in the house at all. Then he recovered.

'Oh, yes. Yes, he thanked me. He said — Yes, that's it. He said, "I hope this won't ever happen again". Those were his very words.' Abruptly he looked much happier. 'And after that I left. So, you see, it was then, on Friday, that I must have put my hands down in lots of places. And that explains those fingerprints. It explains everything.'

They all five sat for some moments in silence. Then Verney turned aside.

'Mr Benholme,' he said, 'you were at the scene when the murder was discovered. Does anything Alec Gaffney here has said conflict with your recollections of the state of things there?'

'No, sir.'

'Then I think this interview might well be concluded.'

Back to square one. Another post-mortem on an interview. Verney's office unchanged. Bar three or four sheets of paper now in what had been his empty in-tray.

But Verney not altogether the same. No snarling rebuke as soon as he had closed the door this time. Instead, shoulders slumped, he made straight for the tall leather chair behind the desk and carefully lowered himself into it, as if he was not quite sure it would be there when he left his full weight on the seat.

'Well, Phil, we made a right cock-up of that.'

He felt a dart of pity for him. Pity for Verney.

'I wouldn't say that, sir. Not altogether. After all, we did find out what that damn boy was lying about, and, if we hadn't, we'd have gone on half-thinking we'd had him in the frame and had had to let him go.'

Verney grunted.

'I don't know that I still don't half-think he ought to be in the frame,' he said.

'Well, I know what you mean. I suppose, technically, we haven't had proof the boy didn't go back into the house on Monday evening. He was in the area all right. He bloody admitted that earlier. But, all the same, that damn silly story about the mouse, it somehow convinced me.'

'Tell you the truth, it convinced me, hundred per cent. Well, ninety-nine.'

'And there's something else, in fact, sir. Something I've just thought of.'

'Yeah?'

'The vomit. The vomit found in the corner of the garden at number twelve, almost certainly sicked up there by the murderer as they were getting away, and Forensic said it had whisky in it. At one time, to tell you the truth, I thought its being there added to the possibility my Conor was involved. I could see him puking his guts up if, in a moment of mad rage, he had done that thing and had had a swig of Dutch courage beforehand. But you remember at this morning's interview, when Alec buying whisky came up, his father said that even the taste of it made him throw up. He was quite vicious about it.'

'Oh yes, I remember.'

Oh, my God. Does he remember, too, that it was when I put my softly-softly question to Alec about his not being able to take whisky that, bouncing in, he almost lost the boy when we thought we had him? He'll scarcely listen to me now if he does.

'Well,' he said hastily, 'that makes it hardly possible Alec was the puker. He wouldn't have been able to keep the whisky in, even if he had taken it to work up his courage. One other indication that we're right in thinking he's definitely not in the frame.'

'All right then, clever clogs, who is in the frame if the Gaffney boy isn't?'

Some of the old Verney intolerant fire back. He must after all have remembered that cock-up of his.

But, as if in reaction to Verney's just-suppressed fire, he found he had an answer.

'Who's in the frame? Well, sir, how do you fancy Belinda Withrington?'

No answer. No immediate answer.

'You know, Phil,' Verney said eventually. 'I've a feeling you may be right. But what's made you finger her all of a sudden?'

'I don't know precisely, sir. I mean, to some extent it was just realizing, I don't know why, that, though we've been saying all along, joking about it even, that this wasn't a woman's crime, there's no reason why it shouldn't be. If the woman had a ruthless streak in her. And if she was physically strong enough to deal out a whacking great thump with that bat. And actually you wouldn't have to be all that strong.'

'No, you're right there, certainly. But go on.'

'Well, I suppose, in part, it was also young Alec going out of his way so often to blot Belinda from the scene. All those times he said "we" and then hastily changed it. You picked him up on it even, sir. And she was all along just as much there in Sandymount on Monday evening as he was. I reckon our Alec knows she did it, and, what's more, he'll know why she went to see the old man.

However much he's wriggled out of saying anything so far.'

'But you don't think, after all, he was actually there? If she was, if she did it. If, if, if, Phil.'

'No. No, I don't think he can have been there. I mean, if he was, he wouldn't have produced that story about the mouse. That only took him off the hook eventually because it was so ridiculous it obviously had to be true.'

'Yes, I'll go along with you there. And I'll throw in something more. Two things, in fact. First, the footmark in the garden. Size seven, could well be the girl. Then the whisky. You know, I see them as buying some, not at that corner shop but somewhere less shit-scared of the law. And I reckon it must have been to give her courage, not him. He said in the end she was the one who wanted it. But this is what we've got to find out: it was to give her courage for what? To go into the house, yes. And I'll bet she left young Alec, too bloody timid to go in himself, keeping watch there in the fog a bit down the road. But why did she go in there? To get money out of the old man, pretty well certainly. But why should she think he'd give it to her? Had she got some hold on him, or what?'

'Can't think of any answer to that, sir. Not at this moment. Nor what would have led to a total row and that yell of *You black bastard*. But, listen, that yell. Mrs Ahmed talked about a boy's voice. Dare say she couldn't imagine a girl doing what I'd told her had happened. But an unbroken boy's voice equals a girl's voice, certainly from that distance away. Must do.'

'Fair enough. But that still doesn't answer the question: why was the girl in there at all?'

'That old Hampton Hoard notion?'

'Might be. I suppose it just might be. Can't say I really go for it though. Bloody unlikely rumour in the first place.'

'Yes. Can't say I much like it either, sir. So we seem to be back to this: what could it have been that took the girl into the house — if she did go in — and led on to her snatching up that bat?'

'That's for you to find out, my boy. And me to learn.'

'Sir?'

'Yes. You to find out, Chief Inspector. Your idea. You get me the proof. You interview Belinda Withrington. Interview her, hard as hard, till she ups and gives us our cough.'

Chapter Nineteen

They fixed on the following day, Sunday, for the interview.

'You're right, Phil. Tomorrow. Sunday. Day of rest. All good parents — Withrington a dentist, right? — got nothing better to do than listen to their little darling being put through it by nasty Detective Chief Inspector Benholme.'

Back in his own office beginning to work out how he might tackle Belinda, it occurred to him that there was now time enough to gather some extra ammunition. Verney had reckoned the girl, failing to persuade Mr Patel at the corner shop to sell her any whisky, had got hold of some elsewhere. Knowing just where might be useful.

He picked up his internal phone, rang down to the Incident Room.

'Sergeant March there?'

'She is,' Jumbo Hastings answered, his voice sounding heavy with a wish that she was not.

'Ask her to come up and see me, would you, Jumbo?'

'Will do.'

A plain note of satisfaction. March been laying down the law again, evidently.

A knock on the door.

'Come in. Ah, it's you, Sergeant.'

'Yes, sir, it's me.'

As much as to say *You sent for me. I've come. Who did you expect it to be?*

He took an instant to control himself. She was the way she was, couldn't help it. Or couldn't altogether help it.

'I've got a job for you, Sergeant.'

She gave him a look in which he detected a clear trace of contempt. I-know-best March.

'Well,' she said, 'since there's no Tarts and Toffs party tonight I suppose doing something's better than sitting on my arse in the Incident Room.'

Oh, God. My cancelling that senseless piss-up still rankling, is it? Well, too bad.

'Right. Well, you remember when you were making inquiries at the corner shop in Sandymount the black lady there said two of my son's friends from Harrison Academy had come in and tried to buy a half-bottle of whisky?'

'I put nothing about that in my report.'

A challenging stare.

Damn. Totally forgotten. She hadn't mentioned it. She failed to see the possible significance. I'm the one who did that. And she doesn't know I was hiding round the corner there listening.

So can I say I was now? Doesn't, as the phrase is, redound to my credit. Eavesdropping. And when I'd been taken off the case, too. Oh, well, come on, admit it. A bit of honesty from me might actually make her think, knock a little intolerance out of her.

'Quite right, Sergeant. There was nothing in your report. But the fact of the matter is: I happened to be — No. The fact is outside the Incident Room I overheard you saying you'd been told to make inquiries at that shop, and, as my son was involved, I took it on myself to go down there, too. Then, hiding round the corner, I heard the answers you got. Including that minor piece of information.'

So, let's see her reaction.

'Did you, sir?'

Couldn't be more poker-faced. But what she's saying to me, damn her, is that she's got something on me now. That she's one up.

Oh, well, let her be, if it makes her feel any better.

'Yes, I did, Sergeant. But what I want you to do now is to go down to Sandymount and see if you can find some shop, convenience store, whatever, where those two schoolfriends of Conor's, Belinda Withrington and Alec Gaffney, did buy whisky last Monday evening. Belinda, for your information, is not quite seventeen but dresses older. She won't have been wearing Harrison Academy uniform. Blonde, average height, well built.'

'Busty, is she, sir? Your Conor fancy her?'

Cheeky bitch. Thinks because I've shown her a weakness she can take liberties with me. All right, but I've got better things to do than play up to that.

'You could call her busty, yes, Sergeant. But Alec Gaffney may be more easily identified. Tall. Six foot at least. Most probably he would have been in his Harrison clothes. And he's got a mop of striking red hair.'

'Then I won't have much difficulty carrying out my task, will I, sir?'

'I hope not, Sergeant. If you get it right, you may even have got us a valuable link in our chain of evidence.'

It took March less than two hours. She was efficient, a good detective, no doubt about that.

301

'Thought you'd like to know as soon as possible, sir. The two of them bought a half-bottle of Teacher's at a shop at the corner of Lancelot Road and Arthur Road at approx. five-forty-five last Monday. People in the place weren't crystal-clear about the time.'

'Good work. You'll let me have your report before you go off duty?'

'Oh, yes, sir. And there's one other thing.'

'Yes?'

What's she keeping tucked up her sleeve now?

'The girl stepped outside the shop and poured a good part of that half-bottle straight down her throat. The ethnics in the shop were jumping up and down about it.'

He would have liked, just to keep March in her place, to have received that with total matter-of-factness. But he could not stifle his pleasure. So Belinda Withrington had swigged down a lot of Dutch courage shortly before six o'clock on the evening of the murder. First-class lever when it came to the interview.

'Did she indeed? Well, well, well. You've done better than I could have hoped, Sergeant. Good work indeed.'

'This is Sunday, November sixteenth,

nineteen-ninety-five. The time is —' He glanced at his watch, checked with the big clock on the interview room wall: '1034 hours. Present Belinda Mary Withrington, accompanied by her father, Mr Louis Withrington, and Mr Barham Williams, solicitor. I am Detective Chief Inspector 2307 Phillip Benholme and with me is —'

He gave the nod to Jumbo Hastings, elephantinely overflowing his chair next to him.

'Detective Sergeant 1017 John Hastings.'

Me, this time, the hard man, Verney's explicit order. Fatherly old Jumbo, the soft. If a soft man's needed.

He went into the appropriate cautioning procedure, looking straight across the bare, shiny green surface of the table at Belinda Withrington opposite. Pebble-hard blue eyes returning his look unflinchingly. Bloody innocent English-rose cheeks, their pink and white not fluctuating for a moment. Tight-fitting jeans at present invisible under the table, together with unblemished brilliant white trainers, checked already as almost certainly size seven although too pristine to be the shoes, one of which left an imprint in the mud at twelve Percival Road. Hanging from her shoulders a denim jacket. Under it a very tight T-shirt, its message *Peter*

Andre Makes Me Randy stretched out to distortion point.

Poor Conor, he thought for one instant. No wonder his adolescent eye had been drawn that way. As no doubt had that of almost every boy at Harrison.

On Belinda's left, her father, the dentist all King's Hampton's top people went to. Fifty-something, squat, hirsute, round jowly face already at this hour dark with beard, thick mobile lips, strong glasses on a pudgy, wide-nostrilled nose. Sitting forward in his chair, a powerful tennis player waiting for the first serve.

And on her right Baa-baa, mild in appearance but with eyes missing nothing.

'Right, now,' he began. 'You know, Belinda, that I'm inquiring into the murder of Professor Edul Unwala, on Monday last, at his home at twelve Percival Road, Sandymount.'

He waited for an instant to see if that got some reaction. The bare recital of what she had done, as he had come even in the last few minutes yet more strongly to suspect, would that, put to her flatly, even produce an immediate confession? She is, after all, not much more than a child still. Despite the sexiness.

He might have saved his breath.

Her expression did change. A little. A quick curve of the lips conveyed *What're you telling me all that stuff for?* No more.

'Now, we have reason to believe that you were there in the immediate area at or about the time of the murder. Can you tell me why you were down in that part of the town?'

'Who says I was?'

So it's going to be defiance, is it? Right, we'll see how long that lasts.

'We have witnesses who saw you.'

'Did they? And who says they were right? There's lots of girls look like me, more or less. Could have been almost anyone those witnesses of yours saw, couldn't it?'

'No. Because one of them happens to know you very well. And has said quite definitely where you were and when.'

'Bloody Alec. He may be more ready to give a girl what she needs than your baby Conor. But I've begun to think he's just another wanker.'

Doesn't care the least bit what she says. In front of me, and in front of her father. Or that she's here being questioned about a murder by a detective chief inspector. No, it's happily getting at me by using what she sees as Conor's lack of guts. But, by God, what I see as his strength of mind and sensibleness.

But forget Conor. Remember I'm the hard man now. Forget Conor. Wherever he is.

Yet for a moment he faltered.

'That — that's neither here nor there. I asked you what you were doing down in Sandymount on Monday evening last.'

'Yeah. And I said: how d'you know I was?'

He jumped in at that. Not bothering to keep from his face the tiger smile he felt leaping to life.

'I know because your friend, Alec Gaffney, has said you were there. And, if need be, he'll swear to it.'

'His word 'gainst mine then, isn't it?'

All right, all right. But you wait, you little cat.

'Now, listen to me. You've got off on the wrong foot, my girl. I'll give you just one chance to put things right. Let me remind you of the facts. There was a murder in Sandymount last Monday evening. We, the police, are investigating it. So we want to speak to anyone who was in the vicinity when it happened. Nothing bad about that. Anybody who was there may be able to tell us something that will identify the murderer.

Now, we have learnt that you were one of those people there. Not just anywhere in Sandymount, but in Percival Road where the killing took place. So, are you going to help us?'

'Don't see why I should. No business of mine.'

'A fellow human being was killed there, young woman. Not only a fellow human being, but one who in his time did a great deal for humanity. A Nobel Prize winner, a man who discovered things that enabled the medical profession to make people's lives better. To save lives. So, make no mistake, it is your business.'

She gave a shrug. An overemphatic, theatrical shrug.

'You say it's my business. I don't. What's it to me, some old man, discovered something years and years ago, gets himself banged on the head? Dies?'

Oh, the callous little bitch.

'Gets himself banged on the head?' he snapped out. 'How do you know he was banged on the head?'

'In the *Advertiser*, wasn't it, stupid.'

Now her father bounced forward.

'Belinda. There's a senior police officer asking you questions, whether rightly or wrongly. Don't let me hear you calling him stupid. You need to learn some respect.'

He came in quickly on top of that, not that her father's rebuke seemed likely to change her.

'Yes, details of the murder were in the *Advertiser*. And they did include the fact that Professor Unwala was killed by being struck on the head. It was with a cricket bat, you know. A cricket bat which the person who killed him took away, covered in blood as it was, and hid under a bush beside Seabray Way.'

A poised pause now. See if at last the recital of what she may have done — what I'm willing to bet she did in fact do — gets to her at last.

But, no. Not the faintest twitch of a muscle anywhere. Tough little nut. Wrapped up in herself little nut. Like a lot of teenagers, of course. They have to learn as they grow older. But this one'll take a long time learning, if I've got her right at all.

'So why were you so interested in what was in the *Advertiser*, Belinda?'

'Who says I was? I look at it, don't I? Sometimes. Saw that about the murder. Why shouldn't I read about it?'

'Perhaps you read about it because it closely concerned you.'

But now old Baa-baa slid in his penny-worth.

'Chief Inspector, are you accusing my client of committing this crime? Because if you are I don't need to remind you that it is your duty to charge her.'

'Thank you, Mr Williams. But, of course, I am doing no more than asking someone who was close by where the murder took place whether she can help us with our inquiries.'

'And I said I couldn't. So can I go now?'

'No. You're not being very cooperative, Belinda. There are more questions I shall have to ask you.'

'Go ahead then. See if I care.'

'Belinda.'

Mr Withrington's round, darkly bearded face went a yet deeper shade of red.

'Oh, Dad, stop interfering, can't you? I don't know what you're doing here. I can look after myself, can't I?'

One for me to answer, I think.

'I doubt if you can look after yourself as much as you believe, Belinda. It's hardly looking after yourself doing your best to antagonize me, for one thing. And it's not looking after yourself by failing to answer simply and truthfully the questions I put to you.'

'That's your opinion.'

All right. More defiance. But defiance of that sort is only there, ninety-nine times out of a hundred, because of what's underneath. And I am going to get to what's there underneath. However hard I have to be.

'Yes, that's my opinion. And it's an opinion you'd do well to take into account. Now, what time did you get back home on Monday after you'd been down in Sandymount? A simple question. So am I going to hear a simple answer?'

A momentary greedy glint in those sharp blue eyes. Some unexpected chance about to be grabbed?

'All right. If that's what you want. It was a few minutes after six.'

Although he was concentrating on her every fleeting change of expression, just out of the corner of his eye he saw squat, ever-waiting Louis Withrington draw back by just an inch or so. The tennis player anticipating an awkward ball.

'Yes,' he said, lowering the tension by way of preparing for what was to come, 'a straight answer. Thank you. And I suppose, when you got in, you had your tea?'

A little contemptuous cock of the head.

'Actually we have dinner in our house. At eight.'

Not good enough, my girl.

'I see. But when you get back from school, you have something to eat then? A snack? Cup of tea and a biscuit?'

'Yeah. Sometimes. And sometimes I just get out of that stinking stupid uniform and into some proper gear.'

Such as this Peter Andre Makes Me Randy T-shirt I've been staring at all this time? Though I doubt if that was what you were wearing on Monday evening in Sandymount. My Mrs Damberry would have had a word to say about that. But we're on to a useful little line here, I think.

'So, right, last Monday. After school you went home and got into your proper gear?'

'Yeah, *gear.* If you like to call it that. Yeah, I did.'

'And then you went down to Sandymount, if I'm not mistaken, with both Alec Gaffney and my Conor.'

'You ought to know. Your son.'

'Yes, as it happens I do know. Now, suppose you tell me what happened down there. You had a bit of a barney with Conor, didn't you?'

Tiny pause for thought.

'All right, yes, I did. He's a bloody wimp, your Conor. Know that, do you? You

311

shouldn't do that, Belinda. On and on, yap-yap-yap.'

'All right, I won't ask you what it was he thought you shouldn't do. But I will ask what time it was when you said whatever you did to him that caused him to flare up and leave you.'

'What time it was? How the hell should I know when he got into his silly bate.'

'Listen. I am trying to establish where exactly you were, and at what precise time. We're interested in finding witnesses, as I told you.'

'Yeah. And I'm not interested. As I told you.'

Beside her Louis Withrington shifted slightly in his chair. Ready to bang in.

'Right. We'll leave that. Since you're unable, or unwilling, to help. But I'd like to go back to when you got home again after your visit to Sandymount. What time did you say that was?'

'I dunno. You got that recorder going, haven't you? Listen to the tape, if you're so interested.'

'Without doing that, I can tell you you said it was a few minutes after six. So you tell me, how did you know that?'

'How did I know? For Christ's sake, how does anyone ever know what time it is? They look at their watch, don't they?'

'Very well. Now, what time does that watch of yours say now?'

Suddenly she looked at the Swatch watch on her wrist.

'Says eleven. Just about.'

'Exactly, please.'

'All right, all right.'

Another look.

'Three minutes past, if you must know.'

He looked pointedly at the clock over the door.

'The interview-room clock reads eleven-oh-three,' he said for the benefit of the recorder. 'Good, your watch seems to keep time, Belinda. Were you wearing it on Monday evening?'

'What if I was?'

'Just this. When you say you got home a few minutes after six by your watch, how many minutes after six was it?'

He turned to look, as unobtrusively as he could, at her father. And found him doubly tense.

So, expecting a lie? And rapidly wondering whether to back it or not?

'I dunno. For God's sake, it was almost a week ago.'

'Oh, yes.' Lower the tension again. 'I can well understand how you can't be sure to within a minute. But you do say it was only shortly after six?'

And before answering she paused to think. Longer this time.

Getting nearer?

'Yeah, just after. Yeah.'

The brief words. The hopefully safe words.

'And when you got in you spoke to someone? Was your father back from his dental practice by then?'

'I don't know. I don't know what time he gets back. Why should I?'

And now Louis Withrington lunged forward. Decision taken.

'Belinda, you know perfectly well. I'm almost always back by quarter past five. You know that. We have tea then, your mother and I. You, if you're there. Listen, you're in trouble, my girl. Now, answer the chief inspector's questions, and answer them sensibly.'

On Belinda's other side he saw Baa-baa Williams purse his lips. The lawyer not altogether in favour of sensible answers. Not when the client may be getting into real trouble.

'All right, let's begin again. You got home after six, right? But just how much after? Remember, this may be important. Important for you. We're trying to establish just how long you were down there in Sandy-mount.'

'I said, I don't know. All right, Mum and Dad had had tea, and I wasn't there then. But I can't remember if I saw either of them afterwards. Or when I did, if I did.'

'And I'm right in thinking you've no brothers or sisters? It's just the three of you at home?'

Louis Withrington took it on himself to answer. To give his daughter time to think? To think that she should answer questions truthfully? Or to think what alibi she might concoct?

'Yes, Chief Inspector. There are only the three of us at home. And, I should add, I myself didn't see Belinda until eight o'clock, when she appeared for dinner.'

'Thank you, sir. So, Belinda, did you see your mother between the time you got in, at six-fifteen or six-thirty, or whatever it was —'

But here Baa-baa did break in. With more sharpness than usual.

'Chief Inspector, my client has told you she reached home shortly after six. I don't think you ought to put words into her mouth. It wasn't six-thirty, she said. Nor was it six-fifteen.'

315

'But what was it, Belinda?' he asked quickly. 'Was it actually six-fifteen? Or was it even later than that?'

'Might have been a bit later than six. I don't know.'

'And you've no one who can help you get it clearer? You didn't see your mother then?'

'No, I didn't.'

The slammed-down answer.

'So, would you like to tell me, having thought carefully about it, exactly what time it was that you did get in?' Little bit of bluff here. 'Let me suggest to you — we in the police make very wide inquiries, you know, when it's a case of murder — that it was a good deal later than six when you actually got home. Well after six-fifteen. Well after six-thirty. Even as late as seven. Yes?'

And he saw the half-second of fear in her eyes. The guess at some neighbour having seen her. His tricky little hint.

'Yes, Belinda?'

'Oh, hell with you. I dare say it was seven o'clock. More or less. What's it matter? I wasn't doing anything down in Sandymount. And you can't bloody well prove I was.'

'No. And we can't prove very much else about your movements that evening, can we? You say now you got home at seven.

But your father's just told us he didn't see you till dinner. At eight. What were you doing, Belinda, between seven and eight?'

'I was in my room.'

'And what were you doing there?'

'My homework, I suppose. It's what they always say I ought to do.'

Again Louis Withrington leant forward. But he was no longer the on-his-toes tennis player.

'Belinda,' he said, an undertow of anxiety in his voice, 'I don't think you were doing your homework. You told your mother, when she asked you, that you hadn't. You said you weren't feeling well. And I must say you didn't look well. So I wrote a note explaining that, for you to take to school on Tuesday, didn't I?'

'All right. So what? A girl feels ill sometimes, doesn't she?'

Then — he could see the idea coming to her, being grabbed once again — she added something, plainly hoping to embarrass her all-male audience.

'I had the curse, if you must know. I had the curse.'

Or was it that you were the girl who sicked up her guts in the garden at twelve Percival Road, and was still pale with shock over what you'd done?

'Very well, Belinda,' he said. 'But are you sure you want to persist with that explanation? I suppose your mother will have some idea of when your period was due. Shall I send and ask her?'

Home.

He could see it. The last barrier but one broken down. The tough line wins.

'Oh, hell with you. No. No, I didn't have the curse.'

'So why were you looking so ill when you came down to dinner, Belinda?'

Would this be it?

For a moment, a fleeting moment, it looked as if it would. But then, for all that the pink and white complexion was now more a whitish-gray, she could be seen pulling herself together.

'Look, you've got it all wrong, Mr Benholme. Yes, all right, I was down in Sandymount later than I told you. And, yes, I was sick. When I got home. But I didn't kill that old man. The — the reason I was sick was I'd drunk too much whisky. I — I thought I'd show Alec what someone with some guts could do. But that was all. That was all.'

Is it all? I don't think so. But neither do I think you're going to break now.

But an hour or two to realize just what

trouble you're in. And then another encounter with nasty Detective Chief Inspector Benholme. After that I'll be very surprised if we don't get our cough.

So before Baa-baa could suggest it, he said he thought it would only be fair to let Belinda think about what she had said. And, like Verney the day before with Alec Gaffney, he added that they would resume after lunch.

Chapter Twenty

Sitting in the interview room waiting for
Belinda, he wondered how well she had
managed to eat her Sunday lunch. Presumably Mrs Withrington, however puzzled or
fearful she was about her daughter being
taken to the police station, would have prepared the customary meal. Or did they usually go out somewhere? To one of the big
pubs, either in the town or out in the country, that offered Sunday lunches, roast beef,
pork or lamb, or perhaps with Christmas not
so far away, turkey? Wherever they ate, he
guessed, Belinda, her sparky defiance
dinted, would not have had much appetite.

What would she have been thinking as
her father cut away at his beef, scooped on
horseradish, plunged the forkful between
those thick, glossily wet lips? Surely it would
have been *When I'm back there, what am I
going to be asked? Will I be able to keep on
and on fighting him off?*

Because he had no doubt now that he

had been questioning the person who, in a sudden fit of baffled rage, had seized that ancient, dried-up cricket bat, raised it, brought it crashing down to kill aged, harmless, tiny Edul Unwala, Nobel Prize winner. For whatever, as yet unemerged, reason.

Partly, he knew, his confidence was mere instinct. But, in the few murder cases where he had led the investigation — King's Hampton crimes were usually less dramatic — he had on each occasion at some point become absolutely certain, despite any clinching evidence, that he had been questioning a killer. And it was the same now.

Not that, he had thought earlier in his office chewing a sandwich, there wasn't plenty of useful evidence already, even if most of it would never be introduced in court. There was the fact that, though Belinda was down in Sandymount the whole of the time the murder took place, she had evaded all along saying why she was there. Then there was her knowledge of the details. She could, of course, have got them from the paper. But in the ordinary way a self-centred girl like her would look at the *Advertiser* only at weekends, for what entertainment was on offer.

Then there were the lies she told about when she'd got back home. She'd grabbed at the chance of getting herself some sort of alibi then, but a bit of bluff had done for that. And why should she have lied unless she'd got something to hide? And finally, there'd been breaking down her silly attempt to throw me by flaunting the fact, which wasn't at all a fact, that she was menstruating.

So, he said to himself now shifting round his chair at the interview table, she's at the edge. I'm sure of that. She's not going to hold out much longer up against nasty Detective Chief Inspector Benholme. Especially when I slip out of my sleeve the business of the whisky traces in the vomit.

Then perhaps the one thing missing will come to light. The why. All right, I'm certain now she did it. But I'm still not at all certain why. No need, of course, ever to know. We get a cough, we don't necessarily need anything more than that to go to court with. But, all the same, I'd like to find out. Why did this wrapped-up-in-herself young woman quarrel with Professor Unwala to the extent of screaming out in rage *You black bastard* and beating him to death?

God knows.

And am I wrong in wanting to know myself? Shouldn't it be enough to find out for certain that the girl did commit the crime?

Isn't that what Verney would do? What he wants me to do? Not to fill my head with the soft man's desire to understand, but to hold fast to the hard man's need to know. To know the facts.

The door opened and he watched them come filing in. Mr Withrington first, once more the bouncy aggressive figure of the morning, full presumably of heartening protein and rejuvenating wine. After him Belinda. Confidence there again, but, unless his eyes were deceiving him, only just. And, trailing behind, Baa-baa Williams, presumably equally well lunched.

They took their places. He switched on the tape, repeated the statutory warning.

And directed at Belinda a squarely uncompromising gaze.

'Now, remembering what I told you about your not being obliged to say anything that may incriminate you, let me ask you this: what was it really for, all the whisky you poured down your throat very shortly before Professor Unwala was murdered?'

The shot went home. He could see it. But after one faltering instant she found that precarious confidence again.

'I told you before. It was just a dare. Show wimpy Alec how to drink. And, even though this naughty girl's under age, you're not going to throw me in your stinking prison for that, are you, Mr Policeman?'

All right. Remarkable what a glass of wine can do in re-inflating the ego. But that's not going to work for long. Not if I have anything to do with it.

'No, Belinda, I'm not going to send you to prison or anywhere else. For that. But I am going to tell you something our investigation's come up with that's not been in the papers. It's this. When we subjected the garden at twelve Percival Road to what we call a fingertip search we discovered, first of all, the imprint of a trainer, size seven.'

He left it there, sure that the implications of *first of all* would be fizzling away in her mind. What was going to come after the *first?*

'All right,' she said, cockiness plainly already undermined by tiny dartings of fear. 'All right, I wear trainers. Wear 'em most of the time. Who doesn't? And, yes, I'm size seven. Like most of the girls and half the boys in my year at Harrison. So what you going to make of that?'

'For the moment, nothing. But, I should warn you, we may want at some time to examine all the pairs of trainers you have.'

Baa-baa stepping in, with put-on infinite weariness.

'Mr Benholme, are you saying that my client was wearing shoes that left a footprint indicating she committed this murder? Because if so —'

'No, Mr Williams. All I am saying is that we need to eliminate, if we can, a footmark we found in the garden there.'

'If you say so, Mr Benholme.'

'But Belinda, I mentioned there were two discoveries made in the garden. Yes?'

'I dunno.'

But now fear was plain to be seen, flickering in her blue, blue eyes.

'But I did, Belinda. I said we had discovered two things that might indicate that you were there in the garden. Two things that need explaining. The first was the footmark made by a trainer such as you might have been wearing. Only might, of course. But the second needs more explanation. It is that someone vomited there in the garden. Vomited only some twenty-four hours before we carried out our fingertip search. And that vomit, so our forensic laboratory reports say, contained a significant amount of whisky.'

'So what?' she answered.

But not quickly enough.

'What indeed? Now, supposing I go on to tell you that the witness who sold you whisky last Monday evening recalls what brand it was you bought. Or, to be precise, the half-bottle of Teacher's Alec Gaffney bought for you.'

He saw yet another flick of fear in those blue eyes.

'And suppose I go on to say that this brand of whisky, Teacher's, differs minutely from any other brand. And that our forensic scientists are very clever people indeed, quite capable of analysing whisky.'

This should be it. It really should. The last, hard blow.

She was silent.

Thinking, thinking and thinking how she could, even now, escape from the tightening circle?

At last she spoke. A muttered response.

'All right, I may have puked there in the garden. I'm not saying I did, mind. But even if that was me it doesn't mean I killed the old man, does it?'

'No. It doesn't. You could, of course, have been there in the house and seen him killed and then started running away and been caught by the horror of what had happened.'

'Yes. Well, it could've been something like that, couldn't it?'

'But it wasn't, was it? It wasn't like that at all.'

He waited. Would this be the moment?

But then in her eyes he saw, if not wholly restored confidence, the fear at least subsiding. So, after all, he'd missed. It had been a sharp blow. But she had managed at the last instant to draw back from it.

'You can't prove anything of that. You can't. I don't want to answer any more of your questions. You said I wasn't obliged to say anything incriminating. Well, I'm not going to say anything any more. You can ask and ask but I won't.'

And, of course, the cavalry, in the shape of Baa-baa Williams, came riding up.

'I don't have to point out to you, Mr Benholme, I'm sure, that what my client has just said is no more than the truth.'

'The truth?' he answered, unable to restrain his bitterness. 'It seems to me that the truth is the last thing we've been hearing here today.'

He had had her. She had been a gaffed fish. She had admitted being in the garden, had admitted vomiting there. And then, when the final question was ready to be put to her — *All right, you were in that room when Professor Unwala was killed, but who was with you, Belinda? Who? I suggest no one else was there, no one* — battered by one hard blow too many she had taken refuge behind that legal safeguard.

The hard man had failed.

Then a thought came tiptoeing into his head. If the hard man had failed, might the soft man succeed?

Give Jumbo, sitting placidly beside him, silent through the whole of the interview so far, that nudge under the table that would tell him to try the other way? The kindness way? And he'd do it well, old Jumbo.

No. No, there was someone else who could do it better. There was soft-as-a-duck's-arse Benholme.

He leant gently forward.

'Look, Belinda, I know how you feel. It's almost as if I was sitting on your side of this table. I know I'd do just what you're doing, if I felt I'd been pressured too hard, pressured too long. But I'd know, as I feel you do, too, deep in your heart, that the way out doesn't lie along that path. You know, don't you, really, that the way out of this terrible mess you're in is, in the end, to admit to yourself you are in that mess. The only way out is simply to tell the truth, isn't it?'

Would it work? If his own truthfulness, the truthfulness he had brought to the questioning now at last, as he could not have stopped himself doing, meant anything it would work. It would.

And he saw that it had. Not completely. But it was beginning to. There had been a quick look that had said *Can I trust you? Will you help me? Really help me?*

He answered to himself, to Soft-as-a-Duck's-Arse, yes, I can help her. Tough nut though she seems, she's still only a kid. The girl my kid Conor felt the flush of adolescent love for. The girl who did, once, respond to that with equal simplicity, equal innocence. So, yes, I can help her. But how? How exactly? What's the key to turn that final tumbler in the lock?

Think. Yes, I must get into her mind. I used to pride myself on doing that. I can do it now. Say to myself *What was she thinking as she went up to that house, in the fog last Monday evening?*

She must have gone there for some purpose. And, yes, of course, that must be linked to her friend, Alec. Alec with her in Sandymount in the time just before the murder, buying her whisky to give her courage. Alec inside that house only a few days earlier. So did he see something there that told him there was money to be got? Belinda's a greedy little beast. She might very well have wanted to follow up whatever Alec had told her. The Hampton Hoard? No. No,

Alec couldn't have found out anything about that as he'd been trying to put that mouse back in its cage, as it had escaped again, as he had finally caught it and then had had to grope down behind the sofa for Professor Unwala's specta—

Wait.

Something stirred in the back of his mind. What was it? Something obscurely connected to Alec groping. Groping. Yes. Had it been . . . ? Could it have been that while Alec was groping for the glasses, he was, yes, being groped himself?

What was it Alec told us Professor Unwala had said when I asked, to help the boy out, if he'd been thanked? Yes, he told us the old man had said *I hope this won't ever happen again.* And, come to think of it, that's not quite what anyone would say to a boy who'd helped him retrieve an escaped mouse. Not with that *ever* in the phrase. Yes, the old man might have apologized for the trouble his mouse had caused. But at most he would have said something like *I trust it won't happen again.*

No, the words Alec repeated, and had been so pleased with himself for repeating, had been what Professor Unwala had actually said. Surely they had. And he had said them, in shame, after having fallen for the temptation of mildly molesting Alec bending down to reach the floor behind the sofa. *I hope this won't ever happen again.*

And, yes, yes, yes, the pair of them, Belinda and Alec, discussing the incident, joking about it, had gone on to concoct a plan to blackmail old Unwala. They had. They had. And, yes again, Alec, the boy Belinda now despised, had not had the guts to go and make his demands himself. So she had said she would. And had swigged back that whisky to give her some final courage.

Yes, that's it. I know now.

'Belinda,' he said, 'let me tell you what I think happened. Your friend Alec didn't have the courage. So it was you, liquored up to give yourself confidence, who went into the house, making some excuse — yes, I think you probably told the old man you'd been taken short —'

In her eyes he saw the instantly responsive flicker.

'Yes, you told him you needed the toilet and then, when you were inside, you simply said that he had abused — was that the word you —'

Now it was more than a responsive flicker. It was a gasp of admission that she was hearing the truth.

He went remorselessly on.

'You said to him that he had abused your friend Alec, and that you were giving him one chance before you told the police. You said if he paid you a substantial sum to show he was truly sorry you would let him off? Yes?'

Yes. He saw the silent answer.

'But Professor Unwala was not the soft touch you thought he'd be. He was a man of determination. And of compassion. He was not going to let you ruin your life by letting you believe blackmail was something you get away with. So he said he was going to tell your parents what you had tried to do. And that was when you shouted at him, *You black bastard.* You were full of whisky rage. You snatched up that bat and you hit him. Once was enough, wasn't it? Once?'

'Yes.'

It was the tiniest whisper.

'Yes, Belinda?'

'Yes, it was like that. Just like that. I did do it. I — I didn't mean to. But he was so — so — so like a rock, standing there, that I lost my temper. A rage. It swept over me. Yes, you've got it right, Mr Benholme. That's what happened. You're right. It's like — It's like you were in my mind, there when it — when I — and you — you understood.'

Chapter Twenty-One

Toffs and Tarts. Bob Carter's postponed fortieth birthday party had been combined now with the customary celebration of a result in a major case. And he had agreed to go. An absurd decision. He could with justice have pleaded that with Conor still a Missing-from-Home, a misper, he was hardly in the mood. But when Bob had asked if he was coming he had at once said yes. He knew why. At the start of the inquiry he had made a terrible error. Letting his dislike of police piss-ups and all that they stood for come to the forefront of his mind, he had banged out his decision to cancel the party. And that might well have lost them their success. So, by way of compensation, he knew he should go now. There would be other major inquiries, and, if they were led by someone seen as soft and unpopular, it could be disastrous.

So, though softness had paid off in the end in the Unwala case, he ought to join in the celebrations, and keep that under his hat. The lads and lasses would not let what had actually happened interfere with their unthinking belief that detective determination always wins.

Well, let them. It was enough that he knew what he knew.

Not that he felt there was anything really to celebrate in his success. A silly, greedy, misguided girl had brought ruin on herself and misery to her parents, had had her name splashed in all the papers, *Nobel Murder: Girl, 17, in Court.* It was hardly something, however much poor little Professor Unwala had been 'avenged', to call for an evening of drunkenness and post-party fornication. But there it was.

But he had said he would go to the party, and, whatever second thoughts he had, go he must.

Only there was the question of an outfit. A Toff's outfit. He certainly possessed nothing suitable himself. Just wearing his old DJ would only label him as being even more out of it than if he had stayed away. And, damn it, even if there were any outfits left for hire after every other male in the CID had had his pick, he would resent every penny he would have to pay.

So there was Mike. He had known all

along at the back of his mind that, once he had agreed to turn up, he would go to Mike and ask to borrow his notorious outfit, tails, topper, monocle, white tie, artificial buttonhole, the lot. He had heard about the kit ever since he had first met Mike. Long before Vicky had set up home with him.

It was a question now only of nerving himself up to make the request. When Vicky certainly, and even possibly Mike himself, would know that this was — no getting away from it — eating humble pie. And more. Worse. Going to Vicky's Mike and begging a favour was saying, yes, you are Vicky's Mike. Or, yes, Mike, Vicky is yours.

But that was the truth, after all. Some day he'd have to acknowledge it some way or another. So why not this way? And why not now?

To the cottage in Frogs Lane.

Where Conor was not. Where he had not been since that terrible night when he had imagined he would find him hanged somewhere, in the toilet at the cottage, out in the foggy darkness of the garden. But where was Conor now? Anywhere. He could be anywhere. Almost certainly not in Barminster or in the county at all. Inquiries there had been as thorough as they could be. But he could well be in London, London the magnet for young people in trouble, where it was more or less hopeless to locate him, however many strings had been pulled. And it being known that DCI Benholme was the man who had resolved the Nobel murder had been more than a little helpful.

But had brought no success.

Time perhaps would do it. One day he might find Conor on his doorstep. Conor aged even eighteen, twenty, twenty-five. Or on Vicky's doorstep. Or in a mortuary.

But in the meantime life had to go on. The files landed in his in-tray. The Toffs and Tarts party was fixed up.

'Oh, hi, Mike. Hoped I'd find you at home.'

'Well, it's where I am. Do anything for you? Or is it Vicky you want to see? 'Fraid she's out doing the big shop.'

'No. No, it's more you I wanted, actually. You see — Well, I wondered — Do I remember rightly that you've got your own outfit for Toffs and Tarts parties, things like that?'

'Sure have. Got the lot. You ever want to be a Naughty Vicar, I'm your man.'

'Well, that's what I do want, actually. Well, not to be a Naughty Vicar, but I — I'm going to a Toffs and Tarts the boys and girls of the CID have organized, and I haven't got any proper gear.'

'Toffs and Tarts, eh? Who'd have thought it of old Phil? But good luck to you, mate. Trust you'll get yourself a nice bit of Tart, keep the old bed warm.'

He took it. On the chin.

'Well, you never can tell. So if I could borrow the gear . . . ?'

'Fair enough, pal. Only thing is, it's a bit difficult to get at. It's stashed away in a trunk in the outhouse now. No room for it indoors, not now Vicky's moved in.'

Go on, rub it in. Rub it in. But, I suppose, you've got a right to say it. To feel it. It's the situation, after all.

'I dare say I'd be able to dig it out, if you point me in the right direction.'

'Oh, yeah, of course. Forgot you don't really know the layout here. But you can't miss the outhouse, straight at the bottom of the garden. Where your Conor stores his treasure-hunting thing.'

'Detector.'

The correction slipped out before he thought.

'Whatever. Anyhow, go along there. There's only the one trunk. Take your pick of whatever you fancy. Key to the place, on the hook just beside the back door. 'Fraid

I've got to rush. Playing Barminster Seconds this arvo.'

'Right then. Well, good luck. I'll lock up behind me when I go. And thanks very much.'

'My pleasure, old man. Old Toff.'

Laughing expansively at his own joke, Mike grabbed a blue nylon sports bag, swaggered off to his car.

He went through to the kitchen, spotted the shed key, took it, let himself out at the back into the dingy winter-bitten garden — one cabbage, brown with frost, alone in its big weedy bed — and walked down to the outhouse.

Key in the lock. Twist. Pull the door open. Pitch-black inside. But there had been a rubber-covered wire dangling from the house to the top of the shed roof. He hunted for a switch. Found it. A dim unshaded light bulb, but easy to see Mike's trunk.

And to see something else, too. Or rather not to see it. Conor's metal detector, which his eyes had instinctively sought out before fixing on the trunk.

Conor's detector not there. Yet Mike had said this was where the *treasure-hunting thing* was stored.

So, only one answer. Conor took it. Conor, going into hiding, had taken with him his metal detector. And that must mean he had been heading for where he would have a chance to use it. And that could only be to Norfolk and that friend he had made at that detectorist camp last summer . . .

But how to get hold of the fellow?

Jesus, can't even remember his name.

Think. Think.

Wait, yes. Surely Conor rang him several times after he got back. Long chats. Expensive chats I wasn't too pleased about. And so, surely, he would have put the fellow's number and name down on the message pad. Yes.

But the pad here, was it the same one we were using last summer? It might be. When I looked at it that terrible night it seemed to be nearly full. So it might well be the one Conor had brought from home. From what had been home.

So, look. Look.

He ran from the shed, skidding on the icy path. Into the house. Sitting room. Table. The pad.

Flip, flip, flip back through the carefully preserved pages. Would Vicky have chosen to rip out that one of all the pages in the pad? Look for Conor's writing. Generally so neat.

Wait. Yes. Yes, yes, yes. Charlie Barnes.

That was the name. And that could be a Norfolk phone number.

It was ridiculously, miraculously easy. He dialled like fury at the old dull black instrument, waited while at the far end it rang and rang. Then . . .

'Hello?'

The cautious voice unmistakable.

'Conor. Conor, it's Dad.'

Silence.

'Conor?'

'Dad. Yeah, it's me. Look —'

Another silence. Not quite as long.

'Dad, listen, I saw all about — all about it in the paper. I — I've been trying to make up my mind to phone. Say I was sorry, and all that. I mean, about — Well, about Belinda. I know I shouldn't have kept it from Mr Verney about her. But — but I wasn't sure. I really wasn't absolutely sure. And — Dad, I loved her. I did. And I sort of still do. So . . .'

'That's OK, son. I know what you mean. How you feel. Listen, I was in love with your mother until . . . And, me, too, I still am in a way. So you needn't feel bad about what you did. Other way about, much as anything.'

'Dad. Well, thanks, Dad. And — and, well, congratulations on breaking the case.

340

Great. Really great. And, Dad, is it OK if I come home now?'

'Of course it is. Of course it is.'

But once more there was that piercing word. *Home*. Who's home would he be coming back to?

'And, Dad, listen. Look, I know it's sort of hurt you, me always saying *home* about Mike's cottage and all that. But, Dad, you really know, don't you, that my home's where it's always been. The old house. I mean, I suppose it is better me living with Mum, and I ought to go back there. But the old place is really what I always mean is home. It really is.'

Seeing things through the other person's eyes. Well, however I've brought Conor up, at least that's there in him. Implanted. That at least.

And now he's coming back. Coming home. No longer that great missing chunk in my life. No longer, as I feared and feared, Conor homeless in London. Sleeping in a cardboard box, shivering, or, worse, a rent boy. That appalling, demoralized life.

But, no. Conor home. Conor, going back to Harrison Academy, getting down to work. It'll take him no time at all to catch up. He'll be as prepared as anybody by next year, when it comes to A levels. He'll do so well Cambridge'll be glad to have him.

Conor Benholme, first-class honours. No, damn it, a double first. Dr Conor Benholme, archaeologist. Dr Conor Benholme, Nobel Prize for Literature, a brilliant book. Father a retired police officer, former Detective Chief Inspector. Never made it any higher, but . . .

We hope you have enjoyed this Large Print book. Other Thorndike Press or Chivers Press Large Print books are available at your library or directly from the publishers.

For more information about current and up-coming titles, please call or write, without obligation, to:

Thorndike Press
P.O. Box 159
Thorndike, Maine 04986 USA
Tel. (800) 257-5157

OR

Chivers Press Limited
Windsor Bridge Road
Bath BA2 3AX
England
Tel. (0225) 335336

All our Large Print titles are designed for easy reading, and all our books are made to last.